GARAGE LOGIC

A Companion
Guide to Life in
the Radio Town

Joe Soucheray

ISBN 10: 1-59298-330-8

ISBN 13: 978-1-59298-330-8

Library of Congress Control Number: 2010925564

Printed in the United States of America

First Printing: 2010

14   13   12   11   10   5   4   3   2

Book design by Ryan Scheife, Mayfly Design
(www.mayflydesign.net)

BEAVER'S POND
PRESS

For permissions requests, contact:

Mr. Joe Soucheray

c/o Beaver's Pond Press, Inc.

7104 Ohms Lane, Suite 101

Edina, MN 55439-2129

(952) 829-8818

www.BeaversPondPress.com

To order, visit www.BeaversPondBooks.com
or call (800) 901-3480. Reseller discounts available.

This book is dedicated to all the loyal Garage Logic residents. It is a reflection of all the good years the GLers have had with each other and the host, Joe Soucheray, who is deeply indebted to all who have made Garage Logic a radio way of life.

For GLers

Contents

Appendices

Foreword

When *Garage Logic* came on the air in April, 1993, I was no stranger to Joe. Sometime in 1980 I heard *Sunday Night Sportstalk* with Joe and Pat Reusse. Those Sunday night shows gave way to *Monday Night Sportstalk*, shows so good that I taped them and listened to them during the week.

Long nights as a watchman at Northern States Power were spent listening to rebroadcasts of Joe's new show, *Garage Logic*.

I don't remember the exact date, but it was around Thanksgiving 1993 when Joe started to describe the physical features of the strange and wonderful mythical town that was developing with each day's show. When I heard about the Knack Hardware and Lounge or the Institute for Cylinder Appreciation I knew I was the guy who could put it on paper and give the town a cartoon life. The characters, real and imagined, events, situations and the always-present dynamic of common sense easily transferred to paper. In this book Joe takes us inside the town and gave me a chance to expand on the people and places that have become real to the listeners.

Wisdom is what Garage Logic is really about. Well, wisdom and fun, but wisdom rules the day. An over-educated intellectual would be more than welcomed in Garage Logic, but if he threw out his lawnmower because it wouldn't start we would wonder why he ever bothered to move from Liberal Lakes or Euphoria in the first place. That guy? That lawnmower? That's a cartoon.

I still have a copy of the first letter I sent to Joe. In it, I claimed that I could make him a millionaire by putting his town on paper. If this book sells a million copies I will sleep well and Joe no longer will need to employ the 48-Hour Rule.

—Greg Holcomb, illustrator and Gumption County Resident

Author's Note

Early in the history of my radio show I interviewed political candidates for various offices in garages offered by listeners for a remote broadcast. Because of my history with garages and a growing realization that the garage is the perfect place to sort through the nuts and bolts of life, not to mention sweat a politician, the radio show became known as *Garage Logic*.

If you are outside of AM 1500 KSTP's signal, or an afternoon time slot interferes with your personal schedule, or you don't like streaming online, you are invited to visit *Garage Logic* within the pages of this book.

In addition to my other duties in the town we call Garage Logic, I am also the mayor.

—Joe Soucheray

Prologue

The American garage, which dates back to the manger, the stable, and the carriage house, has now captured the attention of even the magazines that smell pleasantly of perfumed inserts. Coffee-table garage books are in abundance. Bookstores have a section for garage-building do-it-yourselfers.

The *New York Times* probably offers a half-dozen features a year on garages, wondering about them, curiously, it seems.

It was only a matter of time. Developers, architects, and contractors have effectively exhausted their inventiveness when it comes to the great room and the kitchen and have turned their attention to a new blank canvas, the once-lowly garage.

According to Census Bureau data, twenty percent of the homes in the United States have three-car garages. Floors are either epoxy coated or polished. The walls are insulated and Sheetrocked. Flat-screen televisions and surround sound replace the old paint-splattered transistor radio. Refrigerators are expected. Climate control, ceiling fans, lofts, custom cabinetry, and hydraulic lifts are as common as bench grinders and socket sets.

We are expected as well to know how to organize the garage. Has there ever been a garage feature story that did not show the array of storage systems that suggest neurotic tidiness? After every ride the mountain bike is hung upside down above a modular shelving unit that holds the water toys and the garden equipment. All hoses recoil. All ladders collapse. All rakes and (ergonomically correct) shovel handles disappear into themselves. The same articles paradoxically show a reproduction Skelly Oil clock hanging on the wall. The style setters tend to forget that gas stations of any brand were as grimy as tar pits.

But in featuring the garage as the latest example of cashed-in 401(k)s, or as a pit stop on the interior decorator's charity home tour for the Children's Hospital, the trend hustlers are missing an essential point, or choosing to ignore it because it is impolitic.

In the age of the so-called carbon footprint, we aren't even supposed to have a garage, much less actually enjoy it. Of course, it's in our blood. More politics cannot erase that. Maybe even Al Gore enjoys his garage, as his ancestors have done through the ages.

Old Al Gorg's hieroglyphics scratched into the walls of the cave were early versions of Snap-on Tool calendars. And, from the mouth of the cave, old Gorg watched what was his, stood ready to protect it, saw the coming storm, and steeled himself for what was out there in the night—violent summer storms, deep snows, drenching rains.

The cave allegory is tempting. But the garage connection goes deeper. To nail it down disturbs the political and cultural reality of our time, the yearning for community, or, more curiously, the yearning for us to be a collective. Sometimes it just feels as though we are being rounded up and shoehorned into a country that we don't even recognize.

That isn't who we are. Our resistance is natural.

The garage speaks to a need certainly as primal as the need for shelter. It speaks to our instinctive desire for sole proprietorship, for decision making without committee, for problem solving, for logic and order that has nothing to do with the latest Acme Acu-Tech coated-wire storage bin and the not-very-subliminal message that a bicycle should be hanging above it.

This need for self-sufficiency is as true for any gardener who turns a one-stall city garage into her potting shed as it is for movie stars who park their Ferraris on marble garage floors perched above the Pacific in Malibu.

The garage is where our individuality cannot be denied or legislated, where the games we play and the relationships we maintain are of our own invention, have their own rules.

I went on the air in April 1993. By the autumn of that year *Garage Logic* was created. I heard the word *community* and something happened in the way my synapses fired. The institutions of influence in Minnesota—the media, education, and especially politics—were considerably ahead of the national curve on all the popular crusades: the anti-smoking movement, the admonishment to wear helmets, the disdain for the internal combustion engine, the drive for gun control, for sustainable urban density, for public transportation, for women and children first, for animal rights and organic food.

I knew *community* to mean the old neighborhood or your town, a place with a library and a hardware store and a lumberyard and a gas station and schools and a public square and a bank and churches, too, yes, by all means, churches. But I was hearing the word *community* all the time in a new way, the "anti smoking community," the "bicycling community," the "healthcare community," the "activist community," the "global-warming community."

The activist community? What, they had their own neighborhood?

As for the global-warming crowd, there is always that one question that halts them in their tracks. What is the temperature supposed to be?

They don't mean community. They mean any group of people who identify with each other for purposes of sustaining their victim status. They mean the politics of identity. They mean to be reckoned with as a protected class.

I knew that most listeners enjoyed their lives and were not confined to the dynamics of a particular special-interest advocacy.

For every newspaper article that preached the sanctity of the forest floor, I knew from seeing it with my own eyes that thousands and thousands of people were at Home Depot buying lumber.

For every politician who dreamed up a new tax there were thousands and thousands of us who believed that we were taxed enough and preferred instead accountability.

It gnawed at me that the world outside the studio often felt like a parallel universe. Or, it felt like I was living in the United States but that, all around me, a different kind of United States was struggling to become invented.

What was wrong with the United States we had?

Listeners began sending in items plucked from their children's school backpacks, strange letters and documents of telling significance, boys not allowed to run on playgrounds, prohibitions against the words *Christmas* and *Halloween,* celebrations of the Earth as a mother.

Most of the people listening to the radio aren't driving to the nearest global-warming seminar. They're on their way back from the hardware store or the soccer game, wondering why, if the kid in the backseat knew perfectly well what the score was, the adults in charge of the game didn't post it. And at home they are listening in the garage, likely as not, with the door open to the alley. The fridge is full of beer. If a neighbor drops by, the neighbor knows the rule. The garage beer is as good as his own. He just can't dismiss the brand.

What would it be like to live in a place where the garage symbolized life? Fantastic. Overdue. Familiar in a dreamy way. Our own town, Garage Logic, a made-up place, made up on the fly at first, but a place at once familiar to listeners who dug the vibe from the get-go. Common sense, fun, workbenches, big V-8s that rumbled and thundered—all the metaphors for a life well-lived outside the hectoring call for collectivism and community, a mythical town, with sounds, characters, and landmarks, none more familiar, of course, than the Cass Gilbert-inspired Institute for Cylinder Appreciation at the University of Garage Logic.

Where is it?

Listeners, hungry for such a place, were inventing the geography as fast as I was. To get there you need to find Spoon Lake and head for the west shore. If you reach Indoctrination Lake, you've gone too far astray of the Great Cylinder Divide, the topographical anomaly where cylinder appreciation flows right or left. Double back across the Sparkplug Gap, drop down to Reformed Lawyers Road, and go into Garage Logic on the Common Sense Service Road of Life.

Who lives there?

Garage Logicians live there, of all races, creeds, and sexual orientations. In Garage Logic diversity is a fact, not an inherent value.

Why do we live there?

Because we cherish the United States and do not believe it an unfair or unkind place, and we intend to confront those among us who are attempting to bring about the mystery of a different country, one that is supposedly fairer, less competitive, more collective and, ultimately, meek.

We treasure all the things that the surrounding towns have become frightened of: right and wrong, keeping score, gasoline, cigars, the climate, responsibility, fireworks, individuality. Garage Logicians do not believe the sky is falling and do believe that those who so constantly warn of such calamity have given themselves over to the misguided attempt to invent another kind of America.

With the exception of the absent military, we go to the polling place on Election Day, bad weather making it all the more festive.

We work.

We worship as we choose.

Our bankers regard us soberly before making loans, and we always pay the money back.

We raise our children.

Our students and teams compete.

Just as certainly as The Mystery brews, there is a resistance movement.

Us.

The garage is our headquarters.

One Saturday there was a knock at the radio station's back door. A guy named Greg Holcomb introduced himself, said he was a night watchman who was a fan of *Garage Logic*, and he had drawn a map in his spare time when night-watching was quiet.

"A map?"

"A map of Garage Logic," Holcomb said.

We spread the map out on the workbench used by the station's engineers.

I didn't know what to say. It was magnificent, eerily so. Holcomb had distilled what he heard on the radio into the drawing of an actual town. He would follow that one up with a map of Gumption County, of which Garage Logic is the seat.

There we were on paper, Garage Logic, on the west shore of Spoon Lake, where there is a whopper of a Fourth of July fireworks show every year on the beach, presided over by yours truly, and where on Christmas the Garage Logic Wives' Choir sings *Christmas* carols in the gazebo in the park and people say the word Christmas with the kind of cheerful confidence you don't hear much anymore in the surrounding towns.

I only mention those two occasions because they are examples of when we get together as a town. I would say "community," but we have a genuine Lake Superior foghorn on top of the old tin-man water tower next to the Common Surface Savings and Loan, and it sounds the alarm when it detects words like *community*.

The foghorn used to be out in the countryside, but one of the first things I did as mayor was move it downtown.

Garage Logicians see each other all the time, if that puts minds at ease. We get together now and then, here and there, and people know everybody in town, well, mostly everybody. Besides, somebody's garage door is usually open, even in the winter, and that's where you find knots of the locals, smoking cigars, drinking beer, figuring out the nuts and bolts of life.

We get together formally only on special occasions, Christmas and the Fourth of July, Last Drop Days, the Garage Door Opener, big snowfalls.

They hold us in suspicion in the surrounding towns: Euphoria, Liberal Lakes, and Diversityville. Those places tend to be a bit on the needy side. It's no secret that they like to write legislation and form councils and hold meetings in the schools. In fact, it was in the *Daily Logician* the other day that a group of mothers in Euphoria started a new club, "Mothers Without Confidence," or some such nonsense, because they shared a belief that the birthday parties they were throwing for their children had gotten out of hand and too pricey. The article said they were seeking a counselor to work with them in order to help them control such extravagance.

That made for quite the chatter at the Knack Hardware and Lounge.

I had to go in just to see what was up. Come on in with me. You can meet some of the locals and hear some of the stories that don't get quite all the way fleshed out on the radio, stories about cylinders and snow-blowing, death-defying laser-beam looks, Last Drop Days, and that Harley Davidson that Mr. Unbelievable rides. See it there, parked out front?

It used to be mine.

The First Garage

My first garage was a brown, corrugated-tin shed with a dirt floor hardened and turned into something other than dirt by the oil that leaked out of my grandmother's LaSalle. It was a big, black Series 37 from the late 1930s, a Cadillac, but cheaper, people used to say. By the mid-1950s, when Detroit was growing fins and carving angles, that turtleback LaSalle was already an antique, out of production since before the War.

There was no electricity in my grandmother's garage, no garage door opener. When she got home from the city or from running an errand in the village, she stopped, got out of the car, drew back the wood bar that rested in a catch, and pulled the doors outward on creaking hinges—an old woman doing this, her black sedan idling in the ruts worn between the mossy grass common to Minnesota lake country.

Dust lifted off the floor and powdered the car on its arrival. The engine ticked. The floor settled. The garage then smelled like earth and gasoline and exhaust. And she left behind her own scent, remembered as a part of that whole first garage scene: a faint trail of woman, the aroma of a coat and a leather purse.

I was drawn to the garage almost as much as to the water, both with their attendant primitive mysteries of travel, harbor, and safety. Once, in a storm that darkened the day and produced hail, I raced for the garage and

1

waited it out. It sounded inside like the roof and sides were getting pelted with machine-gun fire.

A ceramic frog squatted on a workbench in the dimness, beautifully painted, a garden decoration that took a hose so that the frog appeared to spit water onto the plants. Remember what the Frog King looked like in *Grimm's Fairy Tales*? A frog like that.

There was a miniature working cannon on wheels, as well as wood ladders, bamboo fishing poles, canoe paddles, oars, a spading fork, ax, shovels, a big ruby-red hailing-from-shore megaphone with a brass handle, a green Johnson Sea Horse on a homemade stand.

Light shot through the roof and sides in pinhole beams where galvanized nails were missing. The dirt floor felt cool and sifted on bare feet.

The service door was sheathed in tin with a backing of wood framing substantial enough to constitute shelving, like a pantry. Here were oil-filled glass jars with metal spouts, coffee cans of nuts and bolts, twine, a flashlight, garden chemicals, fishing plugs and lead sinkers, punks for lighting fireworks, engine elixirs, an oily funnel with a brass screen. On the floor were dark, oily blocks of wood, six-by-six, ten-by-ten, ancient and scarred, always useful in some unexpected way.

My father built our house on his mother's property, and in the process that old tin garage got sold and moved to a farm in Wisconsin, just outside Hudson. I knew where it was.

I trespassed once, on a lark, at night, using a penlight that made out the sharp, spidery teeth of a hay rake. But I could smell the LaSalle and see the eyes of the old frog, and I frisked the shelves behind the door for the now lost artifacts of the mid-twentieth century.

Years after that I could still see that garage, and years after that—well into my thirties.

Then, one day, it finally wasn't there anymore, replaced by a new steel pole barn with electric sliding doors.

Garage Logic

1. A radio show.
2. A discipline of thought and action based on common sense.
3. A make-believe town in the middle of the United States.

Garage Logic is both a town and a way of life. It is the acceptance of common sense, a belief system that anything in life worth figuring out is worth figuring out in the garage.

The radio show *Garage Logic* went on the air April 29, 1993, during a great boom in talk radio, when stations were giving shows to just about anybody: mayors, chefs, musicians, or, in my case, newspaper columnists.

---
*Did you ever think common sense
could be this much fun?*

The Opener

April 24, warm and muggy, the kind of mugginess that could break to the cool side in the spring or get pushed aside by late afternoon sun. What it had going for it was the day, Friday, a potential Garage Door Opener in Garage Logic, the first Friday in the spring to hit 70 degrees.

Just a week before, it didn't make 60, and there was still rotting black ice on Spoon Lake. Burn piles on shore struggled to flame, the leaves still damp with winter mold, leaves and sticks and crud clumped together like cold paste when the pile got stirred by a rake and guys standing in the thick smoke on shore wondered if summer would ever arrive. Two weeks prior, kids still played boot hockey in the slush on the rink behind the high school, and forgotten pucks stood out in the gritty, shoveled banks like wedges of coal in a snowman's face.

Spring was taking its own sweet time.

Not today. Today there was a real chance for 70 and the expectations were growing. The town would go by the official temperature on the clock outside the Common Surface Savings and Loan on Rookie Way.

The mayor, lingering next door at the Knack Hardware and Lounge, came out for another look at two-twenty p.m. 68. If they got lucky the garage doors could be open by the time the kids got home from school.

There were a few itchy trigger fingers in town, and they had their doors already open. No rule against it. If the sun was strong and high in the southern sky there were garage doors open in January. But there was something special about the first 70 and rolling out the grills, the bikes, the muscle cars, the basketballs, and the white legs that hadn't seen the light of day since before Thanksgiving.

The GL Fire Department's one truck, the 1954 American La France, with Buck Aldrich behind the wheel, pulled to a stop in front of the Knack.

"You think?" Buck said.

"I think," the mayor said.

There was a soft, neon *clunk* on the bank sign. 69.

"This could be good," Buck said.

The guys in the lounge part of the Knack came outside, holding beer in go-cups. Darlene was with them, wearing a firefighter's hat that looked even better than when she wore a baseball cap, some women having that look with a ponytail pulled through the back of the cap. Definitely better.

"Buck picked me up earlier," she said, handing an almost-full beer to the mayor.

Another soft, neon *ker-chunk*. They stared at the bank sign.

70.

Life just moved into a different gear.

Aldrich climbed behind the wheel of the old rig. Darlene scrambled onto the back. Aldrich ground the siren in a prearranged series of burpy whoops that signified the official temperature had at last been reached. Darlene pulled the rope and rang the bell. They set off to circle the blocks that gently banked in a tangletown of streets and lanes off the west shore of the lake.

"Listen," the mayor said. But there was nobody around except Two Cycle, the town dog. Everybody had fled home to open their garage doors. The mayor cupped his ear. What a lot of people did on the opener, they had *Frank Sinatra Live at the Sands* cued up to Frank's intro to "Come Fly With Me." It was one of the unknown traditions in town, how that 1966 Sinatra performance with Count Basie made it all the way to Garage Logic as

the official music of the Opener. The mayor, on the sidewalk in front of the Knack, air drummed along with Sonny Payne, Basie's fabulous kicker. Oh, man. Just then the thermometer clicked again, all the way to 76.

76!

Here it came, the Count's boys in top form, Sonny all over the kit and then the drop into the quiet time, Sonny on the high hat, taking it all the way down for Frank, Frank eyeing the chicks at the Sands before he said, now to be accompanied in almost every garage in town on this first Friday to reach 70:

"HOW DID ALL THESE PEOPLE GET IN MY ROOM?"

The mayor wandered home, taking in the cooking smells, the distant shouts of glee, the rumble of cars he knew by sound. Off in the distance, all the way over to Firecracker Drive and beyond, he could still hear Buck grinding the siren and Darlene tugging on the bell rope. Something niggled at the edge of his brain, he couldn't place it. He cut through the alley alongside the Garage Logic Boat Works and onto Curmudgeon Street, his own open garage across the street, the lake beyond. A wreath of grill smoke laced over the water. The chief procurer was grilling shrimp, looked up when she saw him and said, "How did all these people get in my room?"

"That was cool," the mayor said.

Then it hit him.

"Aw nuts," the mayor said.

"What's the matter?" the CP asked. "You love grilled shrimp."

"I left a full beer on the windowsill at the Knack."

"Ouch," the CP said. "A beer crime."

"Yeah," the mayor said, "and on the Opener."

Items Brought Home in a Backpack

The documents and items brought home in a child's school backpack are early clues and signposts as to how the wee ones are becoming indoctrinated into The Mystery over in Liberal Lakes and Euphoria, boys not allowed to run on playgrounds or throw snowballs, prohibitions against the words *Christmas* and *Halloween*, celebrations of the Earth as mother, documents lobbying for yet another school levy, suspensions for those who hug, point chicken fingers at classmates, or accidentally bring onto school property a dangerous nail clipper.

Garage Logicians, who are conservationists by nature, do not waste entire forests of paper on such matters.

Cylinder Index

1. A tabulation of owned cylinders. The number should equal or exceed your age.

The Cylinder Index is the cornerstone of Garage Logic. Nothing distinguishes a Garage Logician from all others so much as the care and appreciation of the internal combustion engine. In fact, it seems axiomatic to us that those who most disdain the automobile and warn against its global harms are the least likely to maintain their automobiles so that they might do the least harm.

To arrive at your index you count your cylinders, dead or alive. A stuck one-lung lawn mower engine on a shelf counts as one, just as the purring cylinders in a new Mustang GT count for eight.

In 1995, a fellow named Paul Schlick brought the index to the attention of Garage Logicians. He suggested the calculation as a means of irritating the officials of the Environmental Protection Agency.

Others believe the Cylinder Index was a response to the clear demonization of the SUV, and still others believe the CI is an acceptable way for Garage Logicians to embrace a garage version of self-worth, without the hugging and chanting and awarding of ribbons that often accompanies activities of self-worth in some of the other towns.

Any reason will do. They are all good enough. It is virtually a rite of spring in Washington, D.C., to have some EPA underling stage a photo opportunity in which she attempts to start a lawn mower while also insisting that just one lawn mower will produce approximately seventeen tons of pollutants. We've done the math. Not possible.

And it certainly is evident that news-gathering institutions, generally, have demonized SUVs, if not the internal combustion engine. With the exception of automobile reviews, which newspapers still paradoxically feature, most stories refer to SUVs and cars as belching, guzzling, and spewing.

It stood to reason that the CI had to develop among people who were neither ashamed nor frightened to celebrate engines that run on gasoline. If new kinds of hybrid energies come along, especially new kinds of energies that allow us to never buy another drop of oil from the Middle East, great. Garage Logicians are all for it.

In the meantime, the internal combustion engine continues to provide us our greatest means of choice, freedom, accessibility, and movement.

It's the irrational fear of internal combustion that most unnerves us. Why, to hear the level of panic out there, you would think that the Earth gets a fever every time some suburban mom starts her minivan. As we have said, we have nothing against new and improved technologies, and Garage Logic has its own tinkerers along those lines. There was a kid at the Garage Logic High School a few years back, Sean Grady, who got his mother's Saab to run on the vegetable oil and grease he collected from the waste behind the First Time Caller Café. The local veterinarian, Darlene Cannon, rigged up an actual sailboat spinnaker on her bicycle so that she goes sailing around town in a contraption that looks like something from a Leonardo da Vinci architectural drawing.

But we also know that Darlene has a good, solid Ford truck for her rural visits and that the Vegetable-Oil Kid—that was what he was called in the *Daily Logician* when Officer Larry arrested him, believing him to be a burglar—went on to do great work under the above-mentioned Schlick, who is the chairman of the Institute for Cylinder Appreciation at the University of Garage Logic.

Over the years great debates on cylinder counts have raged. Do model airplanes, for example, count? Yes, it has been decided. Those little engines combust fuel. Should extra points be given to urban residents over rural residents? Do you get to count company-owned vehicles in your personal CI? Do married couples have separate CI counts? Do we, as Americans, get to count all of the cylinders—billions!—that our tax dollars have paid for?

Whenever a handsome CI gets reported it is natural to ask, "rural or urban?" High urban CIs are impressive and suggest creativity and innovation. City dwellers don't have the space of rural Garage Logicians. It is easier to fill a rural pole barn with two hundred outboard motors and a dozen snowmobiles than it is to fill an urban garage with two hundred cylinders of any kind, even little weed whips.

And the urban loyalist is always fighting a great philosophical battle with many of the neighbors, as the closer you get to the country's tallest buildings, the more likely you are to find people who wish to enact leaf-blower bans because the sound of a leaf blower disturbs them in their hammock as they read the latest UN report on climate change. Our theory is that they just don't want to be shamed into yard work, but they always use "disturbing the peace" as their motivation.

Not to mention that city people are becoming well-organized in their opposition to noise, noise in general, but principally noise generated by cylinders, motorcycle noise, muscle-car noise, lawn-equipment noise, space-management noise.

A Garage Logician settles these concerns by being a good neighbor, but many urban types don't trust civility. They favor, instead, legislation, which they routinely expect—and often get—from their bicycle-riding city council representatives and county commissioners.

It's no doubt tempting to reward high urban CIs with extra points, but it doesn't work that way. It is the cylinder that gets counted, not geographical fate. Despite intense lobbying efforts over the years by city dwellers, the rule has always been and remains that urban and rural CIs are counted in exactly the same way.

As for company-owned cylinders, the answer is no, they don't count in your personal CI. Ownership is implied in all tabulations. By the same token, the owner of a trucking company gets to count all those trucks.

Now, as to married couples having separate indexes, the answer is as complex as marriage itself. Most CIs are household in nature, although there are occasions when husbands and wives insist on their own tabulations for purposes of domestic competition. Those marriages are rare and to be envied.

And counting America's cylinders? There has to be a reason we all love the sight of a presidential motorcade. We own those Cadillacs and Lincolns!

Welcoming Day

Darlene Cannon heads up the Garage Logic Welcoming Committee. It isn't much of a committee. Darlene rounds up the guys at the Knack Hardware and Lounge every time a new family moves to town.

The committee doesn't show up with a gift basket or any literature advertising adult education classes, youth sports activities, recycling guidelines, or the virtues of the Garage Logic Community Center. Darlene and the guys show up because they're nosy and want to see what the new people have brought to town in terms of cylinders.

Roger Holton and his wife Mary are members of the committee now, as loose as that requirement is, and they don't mind the telling of the story of their arrival as an example of what the committee usually encounters on a welcoming day.

The Holtons bought a place out along the 17th fairway at Creature Path Golf Course and were setting up their new home when the committee showed up. Mary still shakes her head in amazement that Denny Jorgenson drove out in his La-Z-Boy, the one with the small block Chevy and racing slicks. He drives it with joysticks on the chair's arms, like a commercial lawn mower.

The first thing the committee saw was the Holton's Ford Expedition plastered with "Love Your Mother Earth" and "Stop Global Warming Now" bumper stickers.

"Hello!" the mayor offered, introducing himself as Mayor, Fireworks Commissioner, and Flashlight King.

Holton slipped his wife a sideways glance and mouthed the words "Flashlight King—what the hell?"

The mayor introduced the Lake Detective, Mr. Unbelievable, Denny from the powered chair, and Darlene, who had sailed out in her contraption that was part bicycle and part sail-bike, a gaff-rigged assembly of mast, boom, and cotton sails.

"We're glad to have you," the mayor said.

Roger and Mary stood together in the driveway. Two children hustled out the front door. Roger made introductions.

"This is our daughter, Alice," Roger said.

"We spell it ALYSS," Mary said.

Uh-oh.

Mary jumped at the sound coming from town.

"What is that?" she asked, clutching her husband's arm.

"We have a foghorn that goes off when it hears a doodled name," Darlene explained. "It's a hard-wired old horn; can't do a thing about it."

"Doodled?"

"A conventional name spelled incorrectly," Denny said. "You'll learn. Say, you got a flat-blade screwdriver handy?" Denny's chair engine was running on. He was constantly tinkering with the timing.

"I, uh, we haven't finished unpacking," Roger said.

"What's the little guy's name?" Mr. Unbelievable asked.

"Robert," Roger said, as Mary looked toward town.

The foghorn sounded, so it must have been Robert with a "y" in there someplace.

"Well, we just wanted to say hi and welcome," the mayor said. "See if there was anything we could do."

"Thank you," Roger said, thinking maybe they could leave.

"And," the mayor said, "we were wondering what your CI is."

"Our what?" *Here it comes*, Roger thought, *a bunch of money-grubbing bureaucrats out to nail the new residents with another tax.*

"Your CI, your cylinder index," the mayor said.

"Look, Mr. Fireworks King, we're not even unpacked yet..."

"Flashlight."

"Okay, Flashlight King, the realtor didn't tell us," Roger said. "We went through the whole truth-in-lending thing and there was nothing about an additional tax."

The welcoming committee loved it when they sprang the big surprise. Property taxes are held enviably low in Garage Logic because the city government has not taken on any extraneous expenses on the order of community centers or bicycle paths, just the usual and expected obligations, like a good street-plowing, a cop on the beat, and streetlights that worked.

"No, no, no," the mayor said, he hoped soothingly, "it's the tabulation of all your cylinders. You'll get asked a lot in town, being new and all, what's your CI? Tell us about your CI."

They gladly admit it now, but that at that moment Roger and Mary Holton didn't know if they had moved to the Twilight Zone. Even their kids, normally rambunctious, being kids, stood absolutely still in the driveway behind their parents. It's not every day that kids see an adult show up on a powered chair or a fellow calling himself the Lake Detective or a mayor who doubles as a fireworks commissioner, not to mention a bicycle-sailing veterinarian and an honest-to-goodness Mr. Unbelievable.

"We can help you figure it out," Mr. U said. "It's what we do on welcoming day. We just count up all your cylinders."

Mary gave Roger an anxious look. It didn't faze anybody on the committee. They were seasoned veterans of the look.

"Tell him," Mary said.

Roger cleared his throat and said, "It's one of the reasons we moved."

"Our neighbors in Liberal Lakes thought we were out of place," Mary said.

"We were the only ones on our block who didn't have an appropriate hybrid car," Roger said.

The foghorn almost shook itself off its perch downtown. Roger and Mary plugged their ears. Alyss and Robert-with-a-*y*-someplace ducked and covered.

"It's not just names," the mayor explained. "The horn sounds when it hears a word whose meaning has become distorted. *Appropriate* and *inappropriate* used to mean 'right' and 'wrong.'"

"It's okay," Denny said, still waiting for a screwdriver. "You'll get to know the horn."

"What's with the bumper stickers?" the Lake Detective said, staring at the Expedition and wondering how it could destroy the Earth.

"Defensive tactic," Holton said. "Until we plastered those things on, the kids in town were leaving us fake tickets on the windshield, citing us for destroying the Earth."

Mr. U whistled.

"Man, let's count you up," the mayor said. "It's actually calming."

"I guess it's okay," Mary said.

"Well, your Expedition is eight cylinders," the mayor said, as the Lake Detective got out his notebook and made a notation. "May we see the garage?"

That is why they really came, of course, scouting treasures and discoveries. The contents of a garage were as good as the tells and tics on a poker player's face.

They had a six-cylinder Honda Accord, Mary's car, she said. They had a lawn mower, a weed whip, and a snowblower. That was three more, duly noted.

"Where are we LD?" the mayor asked.

"At seventeen," he said.

"Say, look at that, in the corner," Jorgenson said, his eye instantly drawn to an outboard motor.

"That was my grandfather's," Roger said, "a 1947 Evinrude."

"That's a four!" Mr. Unbelievable said, making the sound of a four-cylinder engine.

"He does that," the mayor said for Mary's benefit. "He makes engine sounds."

"Where are we, LD?" Denny asked.

"At twenty-one," he said, "and counting, I'd say."

Because, sure enough, there was also a restored 1973 Harley Davidson golf cart for one more, for twenty-two.

"It was my brother's," Mary said, apologetically. "He left it with us five years ago when he moved to Idaho."

"Huddle!"

The committee huddled, invoking the five-year storage rule.

"It's yours to count," the committee said.

They also had a little Honda scooter, the Metropolitan. That put them at twenty-three.

"Anything out back in a garden shed?" Denny wondered. "Like maybe a screwdriver?"

They took the walk. They had a chain saw and a rototiller. That was two more.

"Where are we LD?"

"Twenty-five."

"Not bad, Roger," the mayor said, clapping him on the back.

"Anything else?"

"A boat," Mr. Unbelievable said, already making the sound of a six-cylinder MerCruiser.

A SeaRay speedboat was parked alongside the garage on a trailer, a SeaRay with a six-cylinder inboard/outboard engine.

"You're at thirty-one," LD told them.

They were starting to feel more at ease, and Mary asked, "Does the stuff at our lake cabin count?"

"Absolutely," the committee said.

"We keep a 1952 Chevrolet pickup at our lake place," Roger said.

"Very impressive," Darlene said, for she was partial to pickup trucks when she wasn't sailing her bike.

"That's six more, for thirty-seven," LD reported.

"And a snowmobile," Roger said. "There's another chain saw up there, another lawn mower, and another weed whip. That should be forty-one, right?"

Roger was getting into the spirit.

"Anything else? Come on. Be proud."

"Two old Arctic Cat minibikes!" Robert-with-the-*y* said.

"Congratulations," LD said, "you're at forty-three."

Roger and Mary looked at each other with something approaching fondness.

"How old are you, Roger?" the mayor asked.

"Forty-two," he said.

"Perfect," the mayor said. "You are ahead of your age, always a worthy goal."

"Feels good; doesn't it?" Denny said. "Now, how about a flat blade?"

Make a Move

Making a move is the ability to avoid the drudgery of traffic congestion by always having fallback routes to take for the purpose of keeping moving.

Even if the move takes a little longer on surface streets than crawling along in freeway bumper-to-bumper traffic, you feel better because you kept moving.

The Three Prices You Pay

There's the price you pay, the price you told her you paid, and the price you pay when she finds out the price you paid.

The Second Garage

Urban. One car. Stucco-sided. Set back from the street behind the house and cookie-cutter-matched to its neighboring garage and all the others on the city block, a row of garages consigned by setback ordinances to the utility poles, telephone lines, and lilac bushes.

Nothing distinguished that structure—it seemed to always smell only of automobile tires—except its temptingly pitched roof and its perfect distance from the ground. Perfect for jumping, except for the first flight, when the jolt banged your knees into your chin and knocked you dizzy. You could take a leak between the back of the garage and the hedgerow that separated the neighbor's backyard one street over, a bold thing to do in the middle of the city at the age of seven, but a hardwired requirement of boyhood.

The Mahoney twins lived next door, Bobby and Johnny, my buddies. They had red Schwinns. I had a blue Schwinn. We shared a common driveway between the houses, but they had their own one-car garage. One garage or the other was a bicycle pit stop, bicycles rushed to in the morning and put away at dark, when each garage winked one dim yellow bulb at the street.

One night in the fall my dad told me to go next door and see if Bobby and Johnny wanted to go for a ride and see the new cars. Mr. Mahoney had died a few years before. When we gathered in the driveway my dad told us to get in the car.

The wind was swirling leaves. Moonlight glinted beneath scudding clouds. Halloween was in the air. Me and Johnny and Bobby had decided that we were going out as cowboys.

Suddenly the sky was flaring with the criss-crossing beams of spotlights. The shafts of light seemed to swoop down over the treetops and sail away again into the dark sky. We went to an avenue of car dealerships and stopped at the one selling Fords. The spotlights were on the sidewalk. They made metallic clicks when they reached the end of their arcs and swung the other way.

We arrived just in time to see the theatrical lifting of a heavy brown canvas that had been covering a new Ford convertible, black with red interior. My dad told us to look around.

He ambled off with a salesman. I saw them in the salesman's office. They were talking. They exchanged some papers, and my dad took a brochure and folded it lengthwise and put it in his suit coat pocket. Then they shook hands.

"You guys like that?" my dad asked us when we were driving home.

We were all in the backseat of the car, staring at the magic sky.

"Oh, yeah!"

We pulled into the driveway, and the twins scampered inside their house. As we reached our back door my dad said, "Don't tell your mother."

"Okay."

The Coast Isn't Clear

The mayor only wandered back into the garage in search of a misplaced pair of drugstore cheaters and had no intention of lingering. Birds chirped. Sprinklers hissed. It was an outdoors evening, an open-garage-door evening. He had wheeled a motorcycle outside, but he couldn't see the fuel petcock without his cheaters.

"Do you like this?"

It was the CP.

"I didn't even hear you come in."

She had been doing that a lot lately, not exactly sneaking in, but suddenly appearing in what he began to believe was an odd derivative of the Female Fun-Limitation Factor.

"But do you like this?"

She held a dress to her front, the way they do with the hanger end draped over the left forearm and the rest of the dress held in place by the palm of the right hand. That way they can twirl and show off the garment in the manner of leading ladies standing in front of the mirror after a shopping spree while trying to decide what to wear to the charity ball.

"Very nice."

"I'll say."

Each bike was different. The mayor didn't know if his fuel was on or off. And then he thought, *Too many bikes. Is she trying to catch me in a 48-hour rule violation?*

"Have you seen my garage glasses?"

"Do you want to know what I paid for it?"

The question, of course, is tantamount to begging to be told what she paid so that astonishment might be expressed at her fiduciary shrewdness.

"Uh, sure."

Her right hand flew free of the dress and covered the dangling price tag the way a card shark covers four aces. She moved in for the lesson.

"Well, I've had my eye on this since November. Look what it was in November."

The hand slid one line and the mayor leaned in for the first squint.

"I don't have my cheaters. In fact, that's why I came back in here. I was only..."

"$699," she said calmly.

That snapped him to attention.

"$699! Are you crazy? Have you lost your mind?"

He had ridden to Copper Harbor, Michigan, and back on motorcycles that cost less than $699.

"Now, wait, look what it was after Christmas."

Her hand slid another line.

"I told you; I can't see."

"$499."

"Still seems like a lot to me," he said.

Her hand moved deftly down the tag.

"Now guess."

"What month are we on?"

"March," she said.

"Wouldn't it be out of fashion by then?"

"Not at this price," she said.

"March."

"March," she said. "March it was down to $299."

"That seems more like it," he said, having no earthly idea what more like it might even mean.

"Well, it might seem more like it, but that isn't what I paid."

"What did you pay?"

He heard a motorcycle outside, the *potato, potato, potato* rumble of Mr. Unbelievable's Harley, which used to be the mayor's, but was sold to Mr. U in a complicated arrangement that took in the 48-Hour Rule, the Three Prices You Pay Rule, and the 50-50-90 Rule. It was an exhausting transaction, but they pulled it off rather cleverly. The mayor remained convinced the CP was never the wiser.

The CP shot Mr. U a Quick Glance Look, and he promptly wheeled the bike around and rode away.

"Are you ready?"

"And you bought the dress today?"

"This? No, last week."

That might or might not have been true. Having not previously seen it, that was most certainly true by the 48-Hour Rule. She had him down for the count.

"Ta da!"

At last her hand left the tag, the secretive, guarded, husbanded tag, the oft-marked-down tag, the tag she knew so well and had studied as thoroughly as any scientist studies cells under a microscope.

Once more he had to tell her that he couldn't see the small print.

"I paid $67.99," she said, truly beaming.

"That's amazing," he said, meaning it.

His mind became flooded with questions, chief among them how these stores can stay in business. Or, how much gas was consumed to drive to the mall in Liberal Lakes just to keep an eye on the thing for eight months.

Or, no wonder women say they never have anything to wear. At the price they pay for things, they must feel ultimately cheated or slighted that they aren't wearing something more expensive. And, what was expected of

him now, an acknowledgement, a smooch, a pat on the back? He went for acknowledgement.

"You'll look good in it," he said.

"I don't know; I might take it back," she said.

"You've got to be kidding me."

"No. I noticed they ran an ad for this exact dress in the paper today. It was marked down another ten percent. They should have told me that last week."

She started back toward the house, but stopped and turned.

"Your glasses are on top of the stereo receiver," she said.

"Hey, thanks."

"And don't think I haven't noticed that he's been circling the block. And I know perfectly well that even though you said you needed to sell that bike to finance another one, you ended up with two more, not one, and the price you paid for the second one was not the price you told me you paid because you didn't get enough selling that one to him to finance two more."

She went back inside.

He stared at the closed door for a long minute.

Mr. U, who indeed had been circling the block, drove into the garage.

"Is the coast clear?" he asked.

"The coast is never clear," the mayor said.

The Female Fun-Limitation Factor

The Female Fun Limitation Factor, or FFLF, is a woman's uncanny ability to interrupt garage activity at precisely a defining moment. Just as we are about to start a restored Triumph motorcycle for the first time, the garage service door will open, and we are informed that it is either time to eat or that we have a phone call or that the dog just barfed on the couch.

"No."

"Yes."

At work here is a genetic alarm system that kicks in when the female of the species decides that too much fun has been had, and it's time for the boys to drift back to their own garages. It is not done to be cruel. There is nothing uncharitable intended. The woman simply cannot help herself. She is responding to the firing of ancient neurological signals that probably brought Gorg back in from the mouth of the cave just as he was about to crack another of whatever passed for beer back in the Pleistocene Age.

There have been occasions when the woman, innately aware of her FFLF powers, attempts to at least be playful about it. Seeing what she believes to be her husband's legs sticking out from under the car, she reaches under and grabs him in the, well, the swimsuit area, only to discover that she just grabbed Warren, the neighbor.

If there are a bunch of guys in garages with knots on their foreheads it could be that they got FFLFed under the car.

The FFLF also manifests when a woman, believing herself to be kind-hearted, performs a chore or task involving cylinders that the man has been anticipating with great enthusiasm. No phone call at the office or on the factory floor is more disappointing than the one from the woman at home who proudly announces that she just finished snow-blowing the driveway, or cutting the grass, or sawing up a toppled tree.

"Now you won't have to do it when you get home!"

"Oh. Uh, thanks."

Damn!

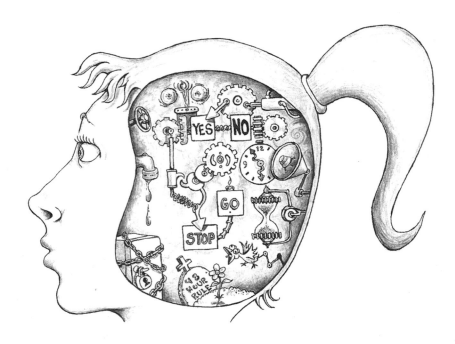

The Look

Women have it as a birthright. The Look is a searing, penetrating eye contact that conveys a thousand words, usually of admonishment after you have done or said something she believes to be incredibly stupid. It also can be issued preemptively, to prevent you from doing or saying something incredibly stupid.

There is no shield for the Look, no distance that dulls it. It can be received over the telephone and detected in a handwritten letter. I know of a fellow who reported that he received a bank-shot Look off a mirror at a garage sale, as he was about to pay a measly twenty-five dollars for an old outboard motor. He put the motor back.

The look even has degrees of severity. The Quick Look is a warning shot off the bow. We survive dozens of those on a daily basis. The Arms-Folded Look must be taken more seriously. Those can sting. The Arms-Folded, Toe-Tapping Look is lethal and usually involves a brief recovery time because, by the time the arms are folded and the toes are a-tapping, you have already done whatever it is that got you in trouble.

Worst of all, of course, is the Burner. That's when folded arms and tapping toes are not enough, and deep from within some genetic reserve is summoned the ability to fire a burning-laser, repeating-fire Look that can singe the skin and drop you to your knees, immobilized, as though you have been zapped with a stun gun. Those are the ones we tell tales about when the women are not around.

It is precisely because of the Burner that beer was invented.

Most remarkably, the female of the species can give the Look from birth. They come out of the chute ready to use this power, and it is not uncommon at all to see a group of, say, four-year-old girls with fully developed Look skills, including all four categories, the Quick, the Arms-Folded, the Arms-Folded Toe-Tapper, and the Burner.

Now, there are women who don't have the power. They come along once in a blue moon, and I don't know what happened to them. Wires got crossed. They even participate fully in garage life, inducing a kind of garage harmony that is so foreign to most Garage Logicians that we step around them warily, waiting for the muted power to suddenly arise from its repression.

These women say things like, "You can leave that running, baby."

I heard that once in a guy's garage. He had started his motorcycle just as his wife's cell phone chirped alive to the sound of "Bolero." In normal circumstances this would be an occasion for a normal woman to issue a Quick Look, and the fellow would shut down his bike instantly. Not on this occasion. She calmly answered her phone and then said to her husband over her shoulder, "Oh, you can leave that running, baby."

Wow.

What was that? Baby? On the grounds that nothing could be that harmonious I could only conclude that, absent the ability to give the Look, she developed other powers as compensation, a command presence that essentially served the same purpose. She was in charge. She ran the show. He couldn't turn off that bike until she told him to.

As I say, that is rare and would take some getting used to. Personally, I prefer the Look because I am used to it, and I have experienced my share of even the Burners.

If I was ever told "You can leave that running, baby," I would think it was a trick. I would start an immediate inventory of my behavior, looking around, thinking I had done something terribly wrong.

Men have tried the Look over the ages. We have tried it, and it's just not there, certainly not with the same powers and ramifications. We try. We even practice in the mirror. But it just doesn't have any conviction.

Besides, even if we could develop the power of the Look, it wouldn't do any good. Just as women have the ability to give the Look, they have what we do not have: the ability to deflect it.

See also: Permission

Quick Look

Arms Folded

Arms Folded Toe Tapper

The Burner

Permission

Permission: The art of listening for and detecting positive audio cues as they might be applied to a purchase, an acquisition, or a desire to go fishing in Canada with the boys.

For example, a woman who comments positively on the color of an ATV, or the bold graphics on a snowmobile, or the reliability of a new outboard motor might as well be telling her husband to get to a dealership as soon as possible. That's permission. The guy can file those comments away. She does not say such things to encourage a purchase, but her words can be used as a defense mechanism if she goes nutso after the arrival of said object at home.

"But you said you loved the color!"

Kitchen Pass: Permission often issued in exchange for housework and applied to activities rather than a purchase, as in: "I got a kitchen pass to play golf."

Sorry, Charlie

One Saturday night at the Knack, Charlie Grady, a typesetter at the *Daily Logician*, announced out loud that he was going fishing in Canada, that it was all set.

"Good to go," Charlie said, beaming.

Nobody would even hint that Charlie isn't at the top of his class. He is as good a fellow as there is in Garage Logic. He gives his time to the volunteer fire department, and he works with the defensive line at the high school for Coach Rolling. He has even helped the mayor as an election judge. You name it, and Charlie Grady has pitched in.

But there is one thing about Charlie. He handled a lot of lead type in the old days at the *Logician*, and there are times when, well, when they worry about him, like the time he launched his fourteen-foot aluminum fishing boat still strapped to the trailer and motored fifty yards out into Spoon Lake before it sank to the gunnels, pulled down by the weight of the trailer. Luckily for Charlie, the Lake Detective was just coming back in from checking his nets for a muskie report. He plucked Charlie out of the water and dropped some diving buoys to mark the spot.

Truth be told, Charlie and Dot had a history. Not that they weren't in love or both extremely proud of their son, Sean, the Vegetable-Oil Kid.

It was a history that had to do with a Look that is still talked about because it was a Look against which all others have been measured and come up short.

Charlie was showing off a bit one day, feeling frisky, they guess. The fellows were at his house helping him paint the interior walls of his garage. They had the Twins game on the radio, and they were drinking a few beers. It was one of those golden, early autumn afternoons when you get the wind out of the south and your ball club in a pennant race and all is right with the world. Why Charlie said what they all heard him say remains a mystery to this day. None of them have ever forgotten it.

About two hours into the project, Dot popped her head into the garage and said, "Aren't you guys done yet?"

Clearly, she was exercising the Female Fun-Limitation Factor, but that's what women do when men paint a garage.

Now, the rules for garage banter are loose. There is plenty of leeway between a man and a wife. But some things just can't be said, garage or not.

"Well, Dot," Charlie said, "if you would've dipped your ass in the bucket and brushed it up against the walls I'd guess we'd be done by now."

What? What?

As the words left his mouth Charlie desperately tried to suck them back in. He stumbled forward, groping the air, like he was batting away a swarm of bees. His mirth turned into fear as Dot entered the garage and positioned herself, hands on hips.

Oh, God, there was a horrible wrath in her narrowed eyes.

The mayor dove behind Charlie's aluminum fishing boat. Charlie's brother Phil rolled behind a motorcycle. Doc Spursm didn't move fast enough and suffered third-degree burns from just a deflected Look. A likeness of Doc dressed in the shirt he wore that day is on display at the Look Wax Museum.

Dot advanced as they scurried deeper for cover. The mayor was dragging the wounded Doc.

Nobody got it worse than Charlie. Dot was shooting a double stunner-scorching Look, the ultimate Burner. It was ricocheting off anything metal,

like flashes from a welding torch. It knocked tools off the workbench, crashed ladders to the floor, caused the motorcycle to actually attempt to start itself. The fresh paint started to peel.

Charlie took a full-frontal Burner and dropped to his knees.

Doc remembered his oath and tried to crawl out to help, but the mayor held him back.

"Stay down!" It was Phil, cowering behind the motorcycle.

Charlie took another Burner that forced him to the floor, where he rolled on his back. His breathing was shallow.

"I've got to help," Doc said weakly.

"No," the mayor said, "you can't risk it."

Dot must have decided to not kill him, to spare him at the last moment. She reversed the categories. She turned off the Burner and went to Arms-Folded Toe-Tapping. Then she went to Arms-Folded, and then she finally left him writhing on the floor with a last glance Quick Look that was painful for its condescension.

As they skulked away they could hear Charlie pleading.

"Dot, you know it was a joke, Dot? Dot?"

"What did Dot say about Canada?" the mayor asked from his end of the bar. "I mean, exactly."

"She said 'Go ahead; what do I care?'" Charlie said.

That swiveled a few heads and they all said, "Ouch."

"That's not permission, Charlie; that's a dare," the mayor said.

"Oh, man," Phinneas Shields from the gas station said, "that might be a double dare because she threw in the 'see what I care' part."

"But the airfare is on sale," Charlie said. "I told her that the ticket is half of what it usually is, half-price from here to Winnipeg."

He had everybody's attention now. They'd all been in Charlie's shoes.

"That didn't work?" Darlene asked. The mayor didn't even see her come in. It would be good to get a woman's perspective.

"She said 'Fine,'" Charlie said.

"But I bet it didn't sound right," Darlene said.

Charlie gazed fondly at the old Hamm's Beer Sky Blue Waters illuminated sign behind the bar, the rippling blue water of a Boundary Waters lake, a shoreline of towering pines. He could see himself fishing.

"It did sound a little flat," Charlie said.

Charlie needed to hear things like "At least the ticket was on sale," or "Who's going with you?" or "Do you even have a license?"

Darlene placed a sympathetic hand on Charlie's shoulder and gave a squeeze. "Charlie," she said, "don't you know what 'fine' means?"

"I thought I did," Charlie said.

The mayor weighed in.

"Charlie," he said, "when a woman says 'fine' she means the argument is over."

"But I told her I was going; I told her everything was all set and she said to me, she said..."

Charlie clamped his mouth shut. He tried to speak but nothing happened. It was beginning to sink in. He had the King Mother dropped on him was the mayor's thinking. Not only had he failed to hear any positive audio cues, but he announced that he was going, the kind of dangerous assertion that can result in a King Mother.

"Did she drop the King Mother on you, Charlie?" Darlene asked gently. She was thinking the same thing. They all were.

Charlie nodded.

Silence.

The mayor took a long, slow sip of Lake Superior Ale. Even the customers in the hardware part of the Knack sensed a great weight descending on the room. They heard the wood floors creaking. They saw a few shoppers whispering, "Dot dropped the King Mother on Charlie."

"Poor Charlie."

"Can you imagine?"

Dot Grady, informed by her husband of twenty-six years that he was indeed going fishing in Canada, said, "Whatever."

It sent chills down the mayor's spine. It takes weeks to rebound from a "whatever."

The Royal Order of 21sters

So long as the sun sets at 9:03 p.m. on June 21, thus creating the longest day of the year, and that the same sun sets at 4:31 p.m. on Dec. 5, making for the shortest day of the year, but sets later by four minutes upon the arrival of the winter solstice, Dec. 21, we, the members of the Royal Order of the 21sters, do solemnly swear to celebrate the arrival of spring on Dec. 22.

In acknowledgement, be it remembered that we have surrendered our membership in the world of the so-called Normal People, and that among our other quirks and foibles is the realization that autumn is a long and lingering season between June 22 and about Nov. 1, that winter is assigned to the dark months only, November and December, and that on our ascendancy, Dec. 22, spring has arrived and that, furthermore, by the time of the Super Bowl, it might as well be summer.

Members in the Royal Order understand and accept that this is merely psychological delusion, but that it works for us to minimize the long and barren months that so chill and depress the Normal People.

Understanding the commitment required and how it is so often accompanied by the derision of the NP, here then, is the Sacred Oath:

I_____, do hereby admit that I am not normal and that I am willingly surrendering normalcy to join my fellow 21sters in the belief, heartfelt, but no less ridiculous, that spring begins before Christmas and that autumn begins before the Fourth of July.

Hooba, Hooba, Gunga, Gunga a Dunga.

Common Surface Savings & Loan

Garage Logicians can buy a lot of stuff for the garage with loose change. They can get a tank of gas for the motorcycle with loose change, too, maybe not the car, but for sure anything on two wheels. Neighborhood kids can be paid with loose change for helping drag a storm-felled tree limb out back so that it can be worked on with a chain saw.

Loose change and occasionally even paper money is often discovered on common surfaces, the ground, for example. It is yours, providing that the surface is, in fact, common. The street and sidewalk are common surfaces. A five-dollar bill is a common-surface find. A bag from the Acme Welding Company containing ten thousand dollars is not. Nobody wants angry welders coming after them.

The floor is a common surface. The ironing board is a common surface, and the change inside the washer and dryer rattles around on a common surface.

Hey, it adds up. In this modern age of pay-at-the-pump, most gas station attendants are thrilled to get a handful of good old nickels, dimes, and quarters. And when you're feeling sporty, toss a few pennies into the common-surface penny bowl next to the attendant's register, a little paying it forward to the next guy.

A bureau is not a common surface, nor is a child's desk, nor is the tray in your wife's car that was designed specifically for her loose change. And the change on your neighbor's garage floor is his common surface, but not yours. His beer is as good as yours, but he buys it with his common-surface savings.

Once Garage Logicians begin banking at the Garage Logic Common Surface Savings & Loan they quickly get the hang of what is theirs and what is not.

That's Garage Logic Common Surface Savings & Loan. There's a branch in every household.

The Fireworks Commissioner

People in town were murmuring. The mayor was too quiet, they said, like he just lost his dog. He wasn't exactly morose, just…off a beat. And here it was almost July.

July was everybody's favorite time of year in Garage Logic. The lake is warm, the skies are powerfully blue, and you can go outside without a parka and snowmobile boots. It was especially the mayor's favorite time. He had long since appointed himself the Fireworks Commissioner, with Brian "Boom-Boom" Cannon as his second in command; Brian, as in the son of Darlene, the town's veterinarian.

There were sometimes a few fireworks at Christmas, and somebody might shoot off a horsetail or a crossette on Veteran's Day or Memorial Day. There was a contingent even trying to spark up Halloween with a few neighborhood Roman candles and bottle rockets, but the big show was always on the Fourth of July, and by late June the planning was well under way.

Brian Cannon wouldn't be working the big show this year, the first one he would miss since he was seven years old. He was killed the previous August when an improvised explosive device, what the newspapers called an IED, exploded near his Humvee while he was on patrol outside the Green Zone in Baghdad.

Back home in Garage Logic, there were no candlelight vigils in the park. Flowers were not left on the street in front of Darlene's house. No grief counselors were required at Garage Logic High School, where Brian had been an All-State tackle for the Fighting Wrenches.

But Brian's funeral was a standing-room-only ceremony in town at St. Mclaren's Cathedral. It was in church, where the candles were lit and the flowers were left in heaps on the altar and men hung their heads in the pews and cried for the kid whose spirit now filled them.

Darlene was given the respectful distance she needed to deal with her unspeakable grief. And because her grief was unspeakable, the people in Garage Logic didn't pretend that they could understand her loss or comfort her.

Darlene knew this, and she knew how the people in town felt about Brian. Every flag in town flew at half-mast through the end of the year. At the Garage Logic Wives Choir performance during the Christmas concert, Dot Grady said eight words.

"We would like to sing this for Brian."

They sang "He Will Raise You Up on Eagle's Wings" before swinging into Jingle Bells.

This was to be the town's first Fourth of July fireworks show on the shores of Spoon Lake without Brian, who was called Boom-Boom for years before he joined the National Guard.

The mayor wasn't down.

He was scheming.

He was planning a second, surprise show for Lights Out Town.

Gumption County is populated with all different sorts, but none more different or mysterious than the residents of Lights Out Town, which has ordinances prohibiting any nighttime commercial lighting in addition to any outside residential lighting after ten p.m. They can't shoot midnight hoops. They can't set up work lights in their driveway to work on a stalled car. They abhor fireworks, believing them to be homage to warfare.

They say they are dimming the lights for the birds, to prevent blinded birds from flying into buildings, and to reclaim what they have been calling "the nighttime sky." But it feels and looks like something else. It looks like a retreat into a darkness of doubt, a cowering from the hope and promise of light.

Dark. So goddamned dark over there, a lightning bug wouldn't fly through town.

If you stand at the edge of Mike Granger's farm field and look beyond at the shallow valley of Lights Out Town, you can see the rheumy yellow glow of automobile headlights, a requirement of the most recent ordinance passed over there, which mandates European headlights of a lower candle power than is common to the rest of the United States. There was a pool going at the Knack as to when the legislative representative for Lights Out Town, Felicia Kram, would attempt to ban cars altogether.

Darlene, who has done some veterinary work in Lights Out Town, never got even one condolence from the valley, not one card, not a whisper of sorrow.

The plan started with Granger. He enthusiastically came aboard after the mayor explained his plan and how it all depended on the use of Granger's property as the staging area.

"Pass the word, Mike," the mayor said. "June twenty-first at my garage. We'll have the meal."

"Bologna, tomatoes and onions?"

"Yup."

"I'll spread the word."

With a staging area cleared he had to plan the actual show, but he wanted to use letter shells, above his pay grade even if he was the Fireworks Commissioner. He needed a pro. He called Stu Aldrich. They met at a fireworks show about five years before in North Dakota. Aldrich gave the mayor his card and told him to call him in the way people do when they don't expect to be called. After listening to what the mayor had in mind, Aldrich agreed.

"Do you need a contract?" the mayor asked.

"How old was this kid?"

"Twenty."

"I don't want a fee," Aldrich said. "I just want to be there."

The mayor would fire Garage Logic's show on the Fourth, as scheduled.

Lights Out Town would get theirs on the fifth.

The mayor spent the days leading up to the meeting on the twenty-first figuring out what they would need to pull it off: vehicles, flashlights, a backhoe, spotters, a silenced off-road dirt bike.

At the meeting, held in the mayor's garage, with the CP bringing in endless helpings of bologna, tomatoes, and onions, the mayor introduced Aldrich. He had shoulder-length hair and a tattoo of a starburst cluster on his right bicep. He could have been thirty. He could have been fifty. Hard to tell. He had been military.

"Your Brian sounds like he was a good kid," he told the group sitting around the feast in the mayor's garage. His voice was raspy, filtered through sand, cigarettes, and maybe a little whisky.

He got along well with the guys, regaling them with his adventures on the road as the pyrotechnic advisor to various rock-and-roll acts, including Paul McCartney and a particularly memorable European tour with Beyonce. It got so steamy in the garage during the Beyonce stories—well, stories about her backup dancers—that they had to lock the door to keep the CP out.

As they talked, Aldrich mapped the show on a piece of cardboard, the front, main body and finale. He marked rack and mortar locations. The front was an attention getter, a laced-together spread of Poisonous Spiders. The main body featured the bloomers, chrysanthemums and peonies, dahlias and five-pointed stars. The finale required letter shells. Aldrich had them specially made, and he would hand fuse them together and fire them off a nail board, a primitive detonator. Old-timers who scoffed at digital electronic firing—usually guys missing at least a finger on each hand—swore by the nail board, an arrangement of nails pounded into a board with wires leading to a car battery.

"The letter shells?" Aldrich said. "They're on me."

The mayor started to protest. Aldrich had already waived his fee.

"On me," Aldrich said, ending the discussion.

"Everybody set?" the mayor asked. "The Vegetable-Oil Kid is on the dirt bike. Mr. U and the Lake Detective are in the four-wheelers to start. Charlie and Mike spotting. I'll have flashlights, and Stu will stage the show."

Aldrich said, "I'll have everything at Granger's by six p.m. on the fifth."

"I'll be waiting," Mike said.

"One more thing," the mayor said. "We don't tell Darlene."

"Won't she want to see it?" Mike said.

"She will," Aldrich said.

The Garage Logic show on the Fourth was spectacular. A larger-than-expected crowd arrived by boat. The mayor could see the red and green bow lights dancing on the soft, easy swells a couple of hundred yards off shore, and some of the pontoon boats were decorated with festive, white twinkle lights. Otto Afterhaulen was out there in his super barge with probably the world's largest American flag ever waved over an inland lake.

On shore the kids were squealing with their sparklers and at the pops and cracks of little Black Cats. Parents had staked out beach and put down blankets. The CP was sitting next to Darlene, both in lawn chairs. Grills were glowing and laughter filled the calm evening. The Vegetable-Oil Kid, a date on his arm, gave the mayor a conspiratorial wink as he walked by.

Full night had arrived.

The Garage Logic Wives' Choir sang "America the Beautiful."

The mayor ceremoniously lit the end of a road flare with his cigar and held the flare aloft. The crowd roared as the mayor set the flare to a fused block of four 100-shot Thunder Kings. *Kaboom! Kaboom!*

But with each touch of the glowing flare to a Saturn Ring or a Happy Face, the mayor was thinking about the next evening and the letter-shell finale they had created especially for Lights Out Town.

July fifth. Two rental box trucks pulled into Granger's place at five-thirty p.m. Aldrich hopped down out of the first truck and released the back doors. A guy who looked like Aldrich and an older guy, his gray hair in a ponytail, got out of the second truck. Aldrich didn't introduce them.

"You'll need another four-wheeler," Aldrich told the mayor.

The mayor called Herb Stempley on his cell phone. Stempley trailered out his four-wheeler and made it in seventeen minutes.

Aldrich supervised loading the four-wheelers, and Mr. U and the Lake Detective set off for the edge of Granger's property nearest Lights Out Town. The Vegetable-Oil Kid had already taken off and was zigzagging between Granger's and the town. They didn't want anybody directly under the field of fire. The CP had fashioned a reasonable looking badge and sewn it on an old Boy Scout shirt. If the Kid encountered anybody asking questions, he was to tell them that the State Department of Noxious Fogging was going to be spraying for mosquitoes that night. The people from Lights Out Town are notoriously accepting of regulatory intervention.

The last item out of the trucks was what Aldrich called "The Encore." He loaded it gingerly into the back of Stempley's rig, and Stempley took Aldrich to follow the others. The mayor walked. He looked back. The two guys who had arrived with Aldrich gave him a little up-nod and then drove the trucks away. The mayor up-nodded them back.

The staging area was on an outcropping of land that someday might grow up to be a bluff. Granger had used his backhoe to dig a trench where guns or mortar pipes now stuck out of the ground like air vents. It was still full light. They dropped the first round of shells into each gun and then sat back to wait. The Kid rode into the makeshift camp and gave a thumbs-up. Charlie and Mike wandered in from the perimeters, swatting mosquitoes.

"A-okay," Mike said.

Nine p.m. Hot. Still.

The mayor had read in that morning's *Daily Logician* that the Garage Logic Police Department had received thirteen calls of complaint from Lights Out Town about Garage Logic's Fourth of July show.

Nine-thirty p.m. The mayor passed out the earplugs.

Aldrich reminded the box tenders to stare at the sky when the box was open. They weren't really boxes, but rather two large, plastic garbage containers with hinged lids that held the shells packed in sequence by Aldrich. As Aldrich fired the shells, the loaders, following Aldrich, dropped new shells into the vacant mortars. When the loaders, Mr. U and the Lake Detective, retrieved new shells from the bins, the tenders, Granger and Charlie, were instructed to flip the lids open while staring at the sky and to close the lids when the loaders said "close."

"You see anything bright falling your way, close those lids," Aldrich said. "I mean, if you even see a twinkle, close those lids."

You could set your clock by what happened next. Below them, about a mile in the distance, the lights went off one by one.

"Ready boys?" the mayor asked.

"Ready."

"Go ahead, mayor," Aldrich said, striking a match to a twenty-minute road flare, "light the first one."

The mayor, who felt honored, touched the flare to the fuse and the ordinance called Six Poisonous Spiders exploded over Lights Out Town.

Each ordinance illuminated Lights Out Town like something seen in the photographic bomb-flash in a war movie. As each burst faded they could see lights turned on, one by one. They thought they heard voices, angry voices, shouting. They probably didn't because their plugged ears were ringing.

They had the town's attention, all right.

Mr. U and the Lake Detective crept along behind Aldrich in an almost musical tempo, returning to the boxes to reload on Aldrich's command. And Granger and Charlie, as instructed, flipped the lids and stared skyward so forthrightly that they later said they missed the show. They stared straight up, not out at the night sky over Lights Out Town. They couldn't risk ignition in those containers.

It was working. A crude, clandestine, hand-fired show, but it was working.

"It's time," Aldrich said.

He had The Encore ready. The nail board looked like something a kid might have made for a grade-school experiment on electrical current: nails and fuses and wires trailing off to a car battery. Aldrich stood and seemed to study the air, to feel it. He had warned them at the meeting that hand-fired letter shells were fifty-fifty at best. The letters could break, or tumble and fire prematurely. They could even bounce, falling back to the ground as duds. He touched wires to the battery. The spark snaked back to the board and caught. The shells spit skyward with a furious whistle. They stopped suddenly and exploded in unison with such a mighty concussion that the men were knocked back into the grass. When they scrambled back to watch they saw the words that now illuminated Lights Out Town in such brilliance that it had to be seen for miles around.

"GOD BLESS BRIAN CANNON."

Holy Christ it was bright!

They could see them down there shaking their fists at the direction of Granger's land, shaking their fists at the smoke ring haze of the words, *God* and *Bless, Brian* and *Cannon,* wisps of white smoke now falling on Lights Out Town even as the fellows were stealing back through the night off Granger's land, The Kid last to join them, snaking back up the hill on the motorbike.

They met back at the mayor's place and cracked beers. They were seriously buzzed, almost slap-happy. They high-fived Aldrich and thanked him.

"It went pretty good," he said, "for a nail board."

"Very cool," the mayor said.

Aldrich flipped open his cell phone and made a call, said one of the guys from the rental trucks would be coming for him.

"The cops will be showing up," Aldrich said, "and I don't want to be here."

The mayor walked outside with Aldrich.

"I can't thank you enough, man," he said.

"My pleasure," Aldrich said. He clasped the mayor's hand.

"Look, Stu, if there's anything I can ever do for you, let me know."

"You've already done it," Aldrich said.

They never saw him again. He drove away just as Larry arrived.

"Got twenty-two calls from Lights Out Town," Larry said. "Seems somebody staged a fireworks show from Granger's place. Know anything about that?"

"Larry," the CP said, arriving as planned. "I made a second batch yesterday. I saved you a plate."

"The meal?"

"The meal, Larry," the CP said. "Come on in."

A hint of fireworks powder was on the air, stirred by a fresh south wind. Larry had left. The crew had wandered home. The mayor was out on the deck overlooking the lake finishing a last cigar when he caught a glimpse of Darlene's sail in the moonlight. He heard the pulleys on her boom and then her cotton sail luffed as she came about and caught the breeze upwind.

She dropped the sail on the beach road and went to the pedals the last one hundred yards before stopping under the mayor's deck.

"You up there?"

"I am."

She got off her bike and climbed the steps and sat down in the chair next to the mayor. "I thought about it," she said, "and I'm not sure you can change anybody in Lights Out Town."

The mayor puffed.

"Not the adults, maybe," the mayor said. "I thought we might reach a few of the kids. I'll bet you right now that we'll have Lights Out Town kids for the Fourth next summer."

She didn't say anything. The mayor puffed contentedly.

Then, "There are a lot of nights," Darlene said, "when I don't think I'm even here; you know what I mean?"

"I think so."

"Not tonight, though," she said, and she suddenly giggled, a girly giggle in the dark. "Man alive, that was a *show*. That was a show."

"We had a guy," the mayor said, smiling in the dark. "We brought a guy in."

"A little mayoral mystery, huh?"

The mayor didn't say anything.

"Thanks, Mayor."

"No, Darlene. That was to thank you."

The CP came outside and sat with them. They sat for a long time in the dark and watched moonlight play on the water.

Bologna and Onions,
Tomatoes on the Side

Harriet, the wife of Garage Logic's champion gardener, Leo, first prepared the special meal for the mayor during a campaign stop at Harriet and Leo's at the edge of town.

"Do you need to eat, dear?" Harriet asked the young political aspirant. "We're just sitting down to a simple supper. Nothing fancy, I'm afraid, just bologna and onions."

"Sure," the mayor said, for campaigning had left him hungry.

Leo came in from the garden and dumped twelve tomatoes on the kitchen table. They were the size of softballs.

"What's this?" Leo asked.

"He is going to eat with us," Harriet said.

"Why?"

"Because he's hungry."

Leo had annually conducted a tomato-growing seminar in Garage Logic, and he did not regard the young political candidate as a prize pupil. "Too much jungle, kid," Leo had pointed out, "not enough tomato."

The smell in Harriet's kitchen that evening was so moving that the future mayor almost wept. What was this simple feast they were about to taste? He took a cue from Leo and wrapped a large beach towel around his neck. Harriet put the concoction on the table. When the future mayor took a forkful he heard the angels sing.

"If you become mayor," Harriet said, beaming, "I will come over and cook the meal for you at your place."

He won, handily, and Harriet made good on her promise. She and Leo arrived on the appointed evening around five p.m. and Leo, per his custom as the town's most legendary gardener, brought with him his own corn, his own onions, and two dozen tomatoes the size of basketballs.

"Good year in the garden," Leo grunted.

The mayor's children were then young. He instructed them to get his slicker.

"The old yellow one," he said,

"Check," they said.

"Almost ready," Harriet said. "We will be using two plates, one for the bologna and onions, the other for the tomatoes. I will feature four sliced tomatoes to start."

She continued to acclimate herself to the different kitchen. She appeared to chant over the meal in a kind of gastronomical gibberish as the aromas began to waft through the house.

"Just a few more minutes," Harriet said.

The mayor's children delivered the slicker. They placed it over his shoulders, like a cape. He sat, quivering with anticipation. The CP placed tankards of ale before the mayor and Leo, in whose huge hands the tankard all but disappeared.

"Here you go," Harriet said, smiling. She was of that great generation of women who do not feel robbed of their station when asked by a man to prepare a simple meal. Harriet called it a Depression-era meal.

It was truly unbelievable. The bologna was sliced and browned, swimming in the sweet onions, the onions cooked so down they melted in the mayor's mouth. The bologna, an inexpensive ring bologna, rose to the occasion, not unlike the memorable flavor of an aged steak or a holiday ham.

As for the tomatoes, the nod was given to Leo, who had won sixteen consecutive Gumption County Fairs with his Juicy Bobs or Lucky Du-Waynes or whatever they were called. It didn't matter what they were called. When the mayor arranged a piece of bologna and twirled around it a strand of onion and next stabbed a tomato slice, the children ducked. The juices were flying. The mayor was practically crying with joy.

"He's eating it all!" the children squealed. "He's eating it all!"

The original tomatoes quickly disappeared. The mayor drained the tomato juice onto the bologna and onions and took a one-minute timeout for a long swig of the nectar. Harriet sliced new tomatoes, and the performance resumed until at last the meal was gone.

"Take him outside," the CP told the kids, "and hose him off."

He allowed himself to be steered, a dumb smile on his face, and stood there as the youngsters soaked him from head to toe. He lowered himself to the ground and rolled on his back, kicking his feet once in the air before surrendering completely to the stupor.

The founding mothers of Garage Logic introduced this Depression-era meal to their children, who in turn pass it along to their children and so on, in the hopes that this simple supper might bring the nation back to the basics of thrift and resolve.

Pay close attention:

A ring of fine bologna must be acquired. Not coarse, fine. If the butcher has to reach around behind him and hook one off the wall, so much the better. Just any kind of luncheon bologna is blasphemy and does not work.

Needed as well is one large, sweet onion and some tomatoes, a heap of tomatoes. These should be from a nearby garden, either your own or your neighbor's.

Slice the bologna into quarter-inch-thick pieces, about the size of silver dollars, whatever. Just slice the ring.

Take a basic saucepan and drop a little butter into it. Drop the bologna slices into the saucepan with the simmering butter, and brown the bologna. There is no time limit. Look at it. Brown is brown.

Next, slice the onion. Put the onion slices over the browned bologna, cover the saucepan, and sauté the concoction for twenty minutes or only until the onions are golden. The sauté process smells so powerfully delightful that strangers will appear at the door. Be prepared to feed them or turn them away. Weeping with anticipation is not uncommon.

At the end of twenty minutes, or when the onions are golden, stir up the contents so that you have a mess of bologna and onions ready to be dumped onto a plate.

The tomatoes are a side dish. They need to be sliced and are eaten from a separate plate. Got that? The main meal, the bologna and onions, are on one plate, and the tomatoes are on a completely different plate.

An ear of corn can also make a nice side dish and a loaf of Italian bread can be used to sop up the juices of the bologna and onions.

Note: Because of its robust flavor and delectable juices, not to mention the sloshing of beer, it is a messy meal. An old rain slicker is advisable, or beach towels might be used as bibs. Upon completion go outside and have a child turn a garden hose on you.

Windmilling

Windmilling is what occurs when activists, usually but not always of the environmental school, are either inconvenienced or believe themselves to be victimized by that which they have advocated for the rest of us.

The inaugural case involved actual windmills to be installed by a private developer in Nantucket Sound.

The Kennedy family, playing the role of American royalty, and featuring among them Robert F. Kennedy Jr., who has championed alternative energy, vowed to fight the proposed wind farm, which might be distantly and vaguely visible to them during a clam-bake when they are on the beach in front of their Cape Cod estate. They think the turbines would be disruptive to marine life, or unsightly, or a yachting hazard...or, well, something that they probably wouldn't have worried about if the turbines had been planned for elsewhere.

The term *windmilling* becomes applicable every time a proponent of a shared or collective phenomenon, particular one that favors Mother Earth, realizes that it will be located too close to them. It can be safely argued that urban light rail transportation has had no greater cheerleader in the media in Minnesota, for example, than Minnesota Public Radio. Why, the thought of Minnesotans dutifully boarding the train with their colorful cloth bags of produce and soy milk practically made them giddy with visions of European sugar plums, except when they discovered the tracks were going on the street right outside their studios in downtown St. Paul.

"We will sue!"

Yes, they threatened to sue on the grounds that the noise and vibrations from the train could disrupt their delicate recording equipment, there being no supporting evidence for that claim, incidentally.

Windmilling does not necessarily have to involve a physical construction.

The American university system is getting windmilled by students who are demanding A and B grades for merely showing up in class or doing what has been expected of them, but little more. The notion that they might actually have to work hard to achieve such a grade went out the window when public education, with the tacit blessing of higher learning, deemphasized grades in order to promote more students through elementary schools and high schools and off into colleges, where they are woefully unprepared to excel but thoroughly indoctrinated in their expectations of entitlement.

Windmilling is, for the rest of us, comedic relief from The Mystery.

The 50-50-90 Rule

When you have a fifty-fifty chance of being right you will be wrong ninety percent of the time.

The Creature

At two-ten a.m., Roger Holton was awakened by his dog's low growl, a guttural urgency that Holton did not think possible of a terrier. The dog was pacing at the window that looked out over the golf course, Creature Path, but moved to the door when Holton entered the room with a flashlight.

Holton let the dog outside. The yard was fenced. He watched as the dog raced the fence line, yelping, and then jerked to a stop to perform a bow.

The next morning Holton walked the fence line with the dog and discovered a tuft of fur in the chain link, a good clump that was the color of dirty snow.

A wolf?

"Why don't you call that Fireworks King mayor of ours?" Holton's wife suggested.

"Couldn't hurt," Holton said. "A wolf is plausible. Hell, a bear is plausible. This place is crawling with wildlife."

Holton let it go, but two nights later the dog was at it again, the same disturbing growl, three o'clock in the morning.

And again, in daylight, another clump of fur in the fence. Holton called the mayor and learned about Lloyd Jett.

"Your dog senses the Creature," the Mayor said.

"What creature?"

"The Creature," the mayor said. "The golf course is named for it. There is a creature out there. We just don't know what it is."

"Maybe a wolf," Holton said.

"Lloyd doesn't think so," the mayor said. "You should talk to Lloyd, Lloyd Jett."

"Why?'

"Why? Because Lloyd Jett, and Lloyd Jett alone, has dedicated his life to identifying the Creature. You should see his garage. It's practically a museum: drawings, plaster casts of paw prints, topography charts."

"That name is ringing a bell," Holton said, "Jett, Lloyd Jett."

"He won the state amateur golf championship when he was eighteen," the mayor said, "right there, at Creature Path."

"That's it!"

"He doesn't play anymore," the mayor said. "The yips got him pretty bad. Well, the yips and a girl. He's a strange dude, doesn't talk much, but you should tell him about your dog. He'd appreciate it. I'll give you his number."

Jett arrived wearing the kind of field jacket that reminded Holton of a cable television news reporter on the scene of a hurricane. Pudgy, bucket hat pulled low over scraggly hair, glasses as thick as highball tumblers. He opened the back door of his school bus. Jett had arrived in a school bus, one of the short ones. He had repainted it a deep forest green.

A hound, a big yellow lab, lazily climbed down, and together Jett and his dog went to Holton's door and rang the bell.

"Jett?" Holton asked.

"Yup, hmm, hmm."

"Why don't I meet you in the backyard."

"Yup, hmm, hmm."

Holton explained the behavior of his dog, the time of morning, the discovery of the fur in the fence.

"Bow?"

"Excuse me, I didn't get that."

Jett nodded at the terrier.

"Bow?"

"Oh, bow, yes, as a matter of fact she bowed, almost like a play bow."

"Yup, hmm, hmm."

Jett's own dog, finding the terrier inconsequential, walked the fence line, occasionally glancing at his master in a way that suggested they shared a form of communication. Jett nodded, and his dog resumed his search.

"I was telling the mayor that I had heard of you," Holton said, "your state amateur title."

Jett nibbled his lip, didn't say anything.

"On this course," Holton said, "*man*, that must have been something."

Now Jett snapped his head, as though shying away from an inside pitch.

Inside the house Holton's phone was ringing, but he ignored it and walked over to the picnic table.

"Uh, here's the fur I found in the fence," Holton said.

Jett turned it over in his hands. Silently, he was able to tell the dog to come over, and he held the fur for his dog to smell and examine.

"Creature," Jett said. "Yup, hmm, hmm."

"A wolf?"

Jett made a face, shook his head no. He was the only person in Garage Logic to have actually seen the Creature—twice, fourteen years apart. The people in town believed with certainty in the beast's existence, but only Jett remained in pursuit, year after year. He had seen it the first time flushed from the pines at the highest point on the course, the green of the par-5, tenth, which he eagled twice the year he won the title, 1968.

He was out at night in a soft sliver of moonlight and the Creature burst from the trees behind the green running off downhill. It was in the winter, and whatever it was spit a rooster tail of snow, ears pinned back. Jett's dog—that was three dogs ago—didn't stand a chance. But Jett was mesmerized. The intrusion was astonishing, for he had always believed he was alone on the course at night, and it unnerved him to think that he had been seen, even by a creature.

The second time, fourteen years later, he was leaving the course when he saw it under a streetlight. It was just a ten-second glance, but it was the Creature: matted, dirty fur, an almost boar-like face, small ears close to its skull, and an awkward gait, like a dog that had been hit by a car and walked with the rear-end never gaining on the front half. He made plaster casts of prints where the animal crossed onto the fourth fairway.

It wasn't a dog, but dogs were intrigued, Jett's own dogs and now Holton's. That bow suggested not only subservience but respect, some kind of laying on of hands that would take both dog and creature back to a shared genetic beginning.

Jett drew pictures and hung them in his garage. He had long since memorized the architectural drawings of the course and came to understand that the animal chose that high ground at the tenth to give it a downhill advantage in flight. And back there at ten, deep in the interior of the course, there was as much cover as in a Boundary Waters forest. You could lose yourself back there, which Jett often did.

Holton waited patiently while Jett took another look at the fur and gazed for a long time at the course, the seventeenth fairway behind Holton's house.

"Yup, hmm, hmm," he said at last, and then he turned and left, his dog joining him in an easy lope.

Holton went back inside. The message light was blinking on the kitchen phone.

"Roger, the mayor here. Just thought I'd give a word to the wise. When you meet with Lloyd I wouldn't mention golf."

In town one noon hour, Holton stopped at the *Daily Logician* and asked if he could look through the library clips. No problem. He pulled the Lloyd Jett packet and began reading. Jett won seventeen youth tournaments before he won the individual state high-school championship three straight years at Garage Logic High School. A state amateur title was not only considered inevitable, but the sportswriters were confidently predicting that Jett would turn pro.

But in 1969, as defending champion, Jett finished fifth in the state am. The envelope dwindled to three remaining clips, one from 1972 when Jett finished tied for forty-eighth in the state am, and two more which did not mention golf but reported that Jett had twice encountered the Creature, and that his plaster casts and drawings were studied by biology professors at the University of Garage Logic who concurred that it wasn't a dog, that it was unknown.

"I've seen Jett out on the course," Holton told his wife, "at least I figure it's him. You can see his flashlight every now and then."

Holton knew his flashlights and suspected that Jett used the SureFire Outdoorsman. Its beam carried a long way.

"I hope he finds it," Mary Holton said.

"Find what?" Holton asked, catching himself, wondering what he meant.

"The Creature," Mary said.

"Yeah, right, the Creature."

One night Holton hopped his fence and started walking the course. He saw a distant flashlight beam swing in an arc. He walked off in that direction, where the course rises to its highest point deep in the interior, number ten. Tall pines framed the tenth fairway where it doglegs left and marches uphill. It was easy for Holton to hang back in the trees.

It was Jett. Jett and his dog.

A flashlight was duct-taped to each of his clubs. Holton watched in amazement as Jett selected a wedge and hit an approach shot that caused Jett to say "Yes!"

Holton moved closer, but not too close. A warning stirred inside him that he was seeing something that he'd best not see, that he should turn away and leave and maybe even whisper a prayer, but he couldn't tear

himself away. He watched as Jett putted, and then Jett noted the number on his scorecard. He picked up his enormous bag, each club fitted with—yes, Holton had been right—a SureFire Outdoorsman and walked to the eleventh tee box and set the bag down. He took out his driver.

Just then Jett's dog bolted into the trees. Holton stood still, watched as Jett turned and followed the dog into the darkness, but Jett couldn't see Holton. The dog came to Holton, stopped, and didn't bark, but gave a cautionary look, let its eyes linger until Holton understood. *Stay back.*

The dog retreated.

Alone, standing on the tee box, just a wink of moon in the inky night, Lloyd Jett teed up the ball and took a few practice swings that tossed the light with an almost strobe-like rhythm against the sky, a beautiful, Ben Hogan arc. He waggled the club four times and then set himself.

"All the marbles, baby, all the marbles," and for a moment Holton didn't know if it was Jett or himself who said the words.

Jett swung, a magnificent, powerful swing, and now it was Jett for sure who said, "Oh, you beautiful thing you, you beautiful thing."

It was a long drive, too, because Holton stayed back and watched for a long time before Jett and his dog arrived at the ball in the dead center of the fairway. Holton froze. For just a flicker Jett played a light back up the fairway, but then bent to his bag and selected a club.

Another perfect swing, the light signing Lloyd Jett's secret signature against the sky.

Flashlights

A Garage Logician takes care of his flashlights the way a big-game hunter takes care of his rifles. None of that rummaging around in a kitchen drawer for the $1.79 drugstore flashlight, which when you find it won't have any batteries in it anyway. When the storm hits you need to be ready.

The garage flashlight is clean and powered up. You know where it is, or, better, where *they* are. It has a purpose. In fact, flashlights are as important as pocketknives, maps, bungee cords, duct tape, long-reach tweezers, WD-40, and magnifying glasses as accessory tools of the garage life. Dozens of flashlights should be squirreled about in various nooks, like reading glasses and cigar cutters.

A good flashlight has a heft. Some of the big D-cell Maglites have such a heft you could club a moose over the head and kill it. Those big Mags make good lake-cabin flashlights, casting a beam so powerful you could guide a boat in through the summer fog. Plus, it is fun at the cabin or outside the garage to say "Who goes there?" and shine a light so bright that the foe is temporarily at a disadvantage.

As flashlight manufacturers search for new markets and market new innovations, they even offer the flashlight as a weapon, with, say, xenon-filled bulbs so brilliant they will blind an intruder. Those are useful.

Mostly, though, the flashlight is a trusty friend, an accoutrement to resolve and efficiency. The inventory should include strobes, fluorescents, lanterns, pinpoint lights on the end of flexible tubes, and any kind of light that can be strapped to the head for hands-free lighting.

A tip of the cap should be offered to O. T. Bugg, who, in 1898, might not have been the first to invent the flashlight but came closest to capturing the hearts of future Garage Logicians. According to *Invention & Technology Magazine*, Spring 2007, Bugg developed a portable electric light marketed as the O.T. Bugg Friendly Beacon Electric Candle. It was a cylindrical battery case, like a candlestick, but with a light on the side.

It was described as looking like a beer stein with a headlight.

Last Drop Days

When the CP came downstairs, the mayor was dressed and ready to go. He had been up for an hour and had already read the *Daily Logician* and circled two motorcycles, a boat, and a Mercury snowmobile in the classifieds.

"Did you have coffee?"

"A Mercury," the mayor muttered, "I'll be damned. Hhmmmm."

"Are you talking to yourself again?"

"What? Oh, uh, one cup," he said.

"Let me see your hands."

He held his hands out over the table. She nodded approvingly. His hands were steady, his shoulders still.

"What in God's name are you wearing?"

"My old Alley Captain uniform," he said. "Still fits, too."

"Looks too tight in the arms."

"Not at all."

Uniforms or costumes of any kind are not required, but the mayor of Garage Logic was looking for something—anything—that would give him an edge. Years ago, when it was his turn to arrange the snow-plowing for the alley, he fashioned a uniform out of an old Northern Pacific Railroad Winter Carnival marching suit.

It was the final day of Last Drop Days, and he had never won the coveted Blue Funnel for lawn mower gas-tank filling. Between them, the CP and the mayor had a dozen or so ribbons for upside-down-ketchup-bottle balancing, toothpaste-tube squeezing and soap-bar reclamation, and one year the mayor even took the oil-retrieval ribbon away from Mr. Unbelievable.

The filling ribbon eluded him as he lost year after year to steadier hands, seasoned veterans who had perfected the art of the cleanest and fastest fill.

A carnival atmosphere was on the wind, a warm and humid August wind. Last Drop Days fall every year between the Fourth and the start of the high school football season, a summer swan song that features amazing feats of saving the last drops of everyday household liquids: gas, oil, paint, varnish, shampoo, condiments. With Garage Logicians so innately attuned to conservation, there has never been a need to establish a town recycling program. There's usually nothing left. The Lake Detective won a blue ribbon one year for building his ice fishing shack entirely from the dismantled packing crates salvaged from behind a motorcycle dealership in Liberal Lakes.

The CP pushed the lawn mower downtown. The mayor, strolling beside her, carried the gas can. Contestants are required to use one-gallon cans, new cans, supplied by the Knack. No funnels or extensions are allowed, just the stubby spout on the supplied can. An ugly disqualification occurred during the inaugural Last Drop Days when a contestant—he has since moved from town—had surreptitiously fitted a tin sleeve into the short stub, but was caught when he cut his finger trying to fish it out at the start and uttered an oath of such profanity that the foghorn bellowed for five minutes.

They had a couple of hours to kill after they dropped off the mower at the paddock, where Larry, the town's police officer, was watching the mowers. He stared at the mayor.

"What's with the outfit, boss?"

"It's my old Alley Captain uniform," the mayor said.

"Looks like something the surgeon general might wear," Larry said.

"I need an edge, Larry."

The mayor and the CP, following their Last Drop Days routine, then went their separate ways. Women tended to gravitate to the household and kitchen areas, and men gravitated to the garage and outdoor division. The mayor knew the other contestants by the guys also carrying gas cans.

The event had grown from simple beginnings, a one-day affair, to now go three days and include beer tents and food stands and a band on the final night, tonight, at the conclusion of the parade of antique and classic cylinders.

Denny Jorgenson, spotting the mayor, wheeled his chair around in the middle of the street.

"Looks a little tight in the arms," Jorgenson said.

"Don't try to get in my head, Denny," the mayor said. "This is my year."

"Well, what is it, anyway? You look like the cover of *Sgt. Pepper's Lonely Hearts Club Band*."

"It's my old Alley Captain uniform, okay, Denny? They wore these in the days when the railroads had marching units in the Winter Carnival."

"Whatever."

Jorgenson roared off in his chair. The mayor stopped at the oil-retrieval garden, an event already completed with the ribbon awarded once again to Mr. Unbelievable for a cleverly staggered arrangement of plastic quart oil bottles, each draining into the one below, and the one below that and finally into a gallon jug, one gallon of oil gained from the final drops in sixty-seven quart bottles. Amazing.

On Paint Can Hill contestants were straining turpentine and varnish through paper filters. Mike Granger displayed a paint-stirring stick he had been using since 1968. Galen Farrington, usually reclusive except for Last Drop Days, displayed thirty paintbrushes, some dating to the 1930s and still in pristine condition. His seminars on how to properly clean a brush were well attended during Last Drop Days.

The lawn mower gas-tank fill was the last trophy event. As the noon start grew near, the CP rejoined the mayor and mentioned out of the side of her mouth that she didn't think the upside-down-ketchup-bottle balancing was up to usual standards, but that Darlene had achieved an astounding retrieval of Durkee Sauce.

"I love Durkee Sauce," he said.

"I know you do, babe," she said, patting his arm.

They were making idle, nervous chatter. With only thirty minutes to go they wandered into the pits for prep time. Contestants are required to clean the tops of the mowers. A spilled drop must be immediately visible to the judge, although it had been years since a spilled drop eliminated anybody. Nobody spills gas in Garage Logic. The fill had become a timed event. The mayor had waxed the shroud of his mower. Most contestants had done the same.

And those mowers? There wasn't a guy in town who hadn't retrieved a supposedly disabled lawn mower during a "clean-up" day in Euphoria or Liberal Lakes, "clean-up" being a euphemism for thinning their towns of even more internal combustion engines. It was astonishing how many Euphorians discarded a mower because it wouldn't start. To think they would get crushed! What would be next, destroying perfectly good cars? It was beneath the Euphorians, apparently, to properly drain a lawnmower carburetor for the winter or clean a spark plug. Give a GLer five minutes with one of those mowers and it would be purring the way it was meant to purr.

With ten minutes to go the general call was sounded. Wives and support crews had to leave the paddock. The crowd moved through town and made a large semicircle around the filling line.

Whistles and cheers filled the air.

"Go, Mayor!"

"Yo, Denny!"

"Holton, Holton, Holton!"

That had to be Holton's children rooting him on, because the town foghorn went crazy.

"Come on, LD!"

"Yo, Denny, Denny!"

And then the cheering was drowned in a cacophony of air horns, whoops, and hollers.

One by one, Charlie Grady, the chief judge, moved each mower into place and asked the contestants for the placing of the cans on chalked marks behind each mower.

"Fillers, get in your gates," Charlie shouted, holding aloft his official stopwatch.

The fillers stretched their necks and flexed their shoulders as they stood behind the gates. Some of them jogged in place, waiting for the bell that would slam open the doors and allow them to dash for their cans. The mayor had drawn an outside gate.

"Bell!" Charlie ordered.

The gates clanged open and the fillers charged. In a choreography of skill and balance, the cans seemed to rise into the air as one as the caps were unscrewed and the cans, in the hands of such skilled experts, were lowered in a practiced rhythm, and the fills began.

"Nooooo," shrieked the CP, her plaintive wail heard even above the shouting and the air horns.

The mayor, his arms restricted by his uniform when he tried to bend at the waist, had attempted to remove his coat, only to get his right arm, his pouring arm, caught in the sleeve of the uniform.

"Take the coat off!" yelled the CP, pressing closer to the fill line.

The mayor looked up helplessly. He not only had to pour from an awkward, upright position, but he was performing the difficult one-handed pour with his off hand, the left. He didn't spill a drop, but he was the last to finish, his last clean, golden drop splashing neatly into the tank even as Charlie was raising the hand of Roger Holton, a first-time winner, who had taken the precaution of wearing an old, loose-fitting T-shirt.

The mayor had suffered the indignity of having been lapped.

"You had to wear the coat," the CP said, shaking her head.

"I should have cut the damn sleeves off at least," he said. "Why didn't I cut the damn sleeves?"

They were alone in the paddock, the mayor having stripped off the uniform. He sat slumped on the contestant's bench, his chin on his chest. There were shouts of celebration from the beer tent.

"Come on, captain," the CP said, taking his hand and tugging him off the bench, "Roger is buying. Maybe he'll let you take a swig from the Blue Funnel."

"I would have bought, too," the mayor said.

"I know you would have, babe. I know."

The Third Garage

It sat approximately where the First Garage had been, but it was modern and expansive and agreeably captured the suburban sprawl of the 1960s. By design it wasn't much, but it had an oversized two-car section and an adjoining one-stall with a ten-foot-wide door. Plenty wide, and deep, too, twenty-five feet deep.

There were rafters, accessed by a ladder. A few pieces from the First Garage were up there, principally a megaphone that apparently was as difficult to throw away as a good block of wood. There was a table radio up there and a tricycle the likes of which I have not seen since. It was humongous. I secretly believed that in the annals of the family we must have had somebody confined by a medical condition to a large tricycle. Either that or the family went through a period where they had a tricycle-riding circus bear.

In the summer it was a playhouse, a Chautauqua, for a mess of sisters who scored their own musicals and then out-screeched each other at the soup-can microphone taped to the end of a broomstick. They loved *Cinderella* and fought to play her, planting Cinderella's script in the mop bucket so they could glimpse her lines. They did *The Sound of Music* and *West Side Story*. These occasions demanded the printing of tickets and an arrangement of benches and chairs in the circular driveway. A concession stand consisted of watered-down Kool-Aid and stale popcorn.

It never bothered the actresses that, simultaneous to the second act, the grass might be getting cut.

On the arrival of new neighbors, two doors down, garage rock-and-roll was born. The new people brought with them, from Indiana, a drum set. I saw them carrying it into the house. I saw it because a golden shaft of light beamed down from the heavens and sparkled and glinted off the bass drum. The bass drum was red and evoked the Civil War, a great big thumper with brass tuning thumbscrews. The minute I saw that drum, my jaw dropped and my knees trembled. They put it in their basement. For weeks after their arrival I stared at the drum through their basement windows.

One of the new kids, Lila, caught me.

"Whatcha looking at?"

"Dududududududu...."

I couldn't talk.

"Huh?"

"Dddddrum," I managed to stammer.

"Oh, those old things," Lila said. "I'll ask my parents."

I had to get Lila a role in next year's garage musical, but I got the drums. At the time I might have been the least rhythmic white person in the United States, but when I saw those drums I thought they were the key to coolness. My buddies and I put a band together and practiced all winter in the basement, but we were cramped in the basement and couldn't wait to spread out in the garage and hear what we really sounded like in full fury.

We never announced the first performance. We just started playing one summer night and the crowd, admittedly bolstered by the population at the neighboring public beach, spread out into the street to the point where somebody must have called Swede, the town cop.

Swede drove slowly through the crowd and burped his siren. We kept playing. Swede stopped and got out of the car and found my father.

"What have you got here, Henry?"

Henry was raised on opera music and said, "Damned if I know."

"Cinderella didn't draw this kind of crowd," Swede said. "Tell them to wrap it up by ten p.m."

You could get a bicycle fixed in that garage and then hear the everlasting plaintive wail of fatherhood: "Put those tools back where they belong!" You could shoot hockey pucks in there, too, and I think Henry had to look the other way on those dents that pockmarked the interior fiberboard when the makeshift nets were missed by killer slapshots and nifty backhands.

Despite the plays and the hockey players and the rock-and-rollers it was still a garage, wholly accommodating of America's growing needs and pursuits. The charms of a Model A Ford got discovered, then MGs, a 1941 Plymouth, and a 1955 Ford pickup truck nicknamed "Haul It."

In other words, it was a shrine to gasoline, gas, "gaz." That's the way it got pronounced once in a while: "Get me some gaz." My father flew the Hump in India during World War II. As I understand it—he died before my generation thought to grill their fathers about World War II—he was in a crew that flew drums of gasoline through the Aluminum Highway on C-47 Transports. He was not at all a demonstrative guy, or superstitious, but I always wondered if maybe he developed a bond with fuel, possibly as a result of not having been blown up by it.

We had a lot of gaz, man. It was snappy to hear it said that way, hip.

There were six or seven containers of various capacities. The yard equipment division alone featured old lawn mowers, a primitive yard tractor from Ward's, and a snowblower as big as a Volkswagen. Throw in a marine division with a couple of outboard motors and factor in the cars, and you had significant fuel requirements.

Gas was a fuel, a cleaning agent, a weed killer, a lubricant, a fire starter, a lifeline, and a sweet, sweet smell on a grass-cutting morning.

Gaz.

Halloween

The old wood floors of the Knack Hardware and Lounge creaked and groaned under the weight of the guys buying hardware. Only three days to go before Halloween, and the guys had decided this year was a chug year. A chug is a home-built downhill-racing car with a steerable front end. Usually the kid steers it with a rope, or his feet, when they race the carts down Spoon Lake Hill. Some of the chugs get elaborate and end up looking like Barney Oldfield's Indy 500 racecars.

"What is it is this year?" the guys would ask each other at the Knack or around town.

"Chug is what I heard."

The Royal Order of the 21sters makes the decision every year as part of the summer meeting. The 21sters are the people in Garage Logic who lament June 21st as the longest day of the year because the days then start getting shorter, but who celebrate Dec. 22 as the first day of spring because the days start to get longer. The 21sters understand that it is psychological trickery, but it gets them through the two dark months they assign to winter, November and December. Halloween, in the scheme of the order's delusion, is the last day of fall and deserving of a unique twist on the tradition.

The kids in GL trick-or-treat for candy at the front door, just like kids everywhere. But when they go around back and find an open garage door

they trick or treat for hardware. Real hardware: fasteners, nuts, bolts, washers, screws, nails, small tools, steel rods, rubber wagon wheels. Give a kid a Snicker bar, and he eats it once. But give a kid a set of stainless steel nuts and bolts, and the kid is hooked for life.

Not everybody participates. Galen Farrington never has his garage door open, but when he heard about the chugs he said he would leave the garage light on and set out a pile of wood scraps for the kids to pick through.

The first three kids at the mayor's garage were cowboys, complete with six-shooters in holsters.

"Trick or treat, Mayor," they said.

"Give me a shot or two," the mayor said.

All three cowboys drew their pistols and fired rapid cap-gun bursts. Then they blew smoke across the barrels and reholstered.

"Not bad," the mayor said. "You know what caps are, right?"

The cowboys rolled their eyes. The mayor put them through this every year.

"Of course we know. They're beginner fireworks."

The mayor gave them each a set of nuts, bolts, and washers suitable for securing wheels to a two-by-four and two steel rods, axels.

"A chug, huh?" The kids instinctively knew.

"A chug this year," the mayor said."

"Cool."

"Mr. Farrington left some wood out," the mayor said.

The cowpokes quickly disappeared into the night. Those kids would tell others, and they would tell others, and it wouldn't be long before all the kids in town knew what they would be doing with the collection of hardware.

The 21sters figured the expenditure was worth it. It had been their experience that if you get a kid hooked early to the ways of the garage the kid usually turned out all right in life. It is statistically impossible to find anybody in prison, for example, who, as a kid, got hardware for Halloween. And Pete Young at the Knack couldn't be happier. He owned a place in the Florida Keys and wasn't shy about insisting that it was all due to the week before Halloween, when he had his biggest sales of the year, bigger than even Christmas.

Hundreds of cowboys, pirates, hobos, and ballerinas were wandering the streets. A snappy wind blew in off the lake. Leaves swirled. Smoke from fire pits drifted. It was candy at the front door and business at the back. A kid saw some amazing things on Halloween night, restored Model A Fords, dismantled snowmobiles, working steam engines, outboard motors running in fifty-gallon drums of water. The guys had their best cylinders running and polished for Halloween, and they were out in the streets, too, keeping an eye on things while showing off their cylinders.

Halloween was usually trouble-free, but it didn't hurt for adults to at least be visible. The foghorn could cause immense curiosity, and once in a while a kid had to be rescued from the water tower. And a couple of years previously, the Mahoney twins went into a six-plex in Liberal Lakes and came out with a sealed bottle of Canadian Club whisky dropped into Bobby

Mahoney's bag. Mr. and Mrs. Mahoney wrestled for the bottle on the living room floor after the twins dumped their bags for inspection. Mr. Mahoney enjoyed a brief lead in points before Mrs. Mahoney flipped him with a nifty scissors kick and emerged from the scrum with the bottle, which she promptly poured in the kitchen sink.

From that whisky year on, more and more machinery began to appear on the streets.

The mayor always lingered outside, waiting to play his mailbox trick. When he saw unsuspecting youngsters approaching he ducked into the garage and knocked three times on the inner wall. That alerted the CP. When the kids came to the door, the CP deposited the bounty and then, feigning forgetfulness, asked them if they would retrieve her mail from the slot on the side of the garage.

"Sure thing."

The mayor, crouched, lurking, would grab the first hand through the slot and the kid would jump six feet into the air. Occasionally, the mayor had to step outside and soothe an outraged parent who was waiting at the curb.

Mr. Unbelievable, wearing a Frankenstein mask, swung by the mayor's garage on his primitive, fat-tired three-wheeler, the precursor of today's modern off-road four-wheelers. Mr. U's contraption didn't even have suspension. The air in the fat tires dampened the ride. It was impossible to steer; you couldn't tow anything with it, but it was another cylinder to count.

"Those cowboys?" Mr. U asked, a cigarette sticking out of the mask's mouth.

"Yeah."

"They got me for three complete sets of wheels. Is Pete still open?

"'Til eight," the mayor said.

Mr. U took off for town.

"Hey," the mayor yelled after him, "get me some more axels."

Parked in front of the Knack was a go-cart, Denny Jorgenson's V-8 powered chair, Herb Stempley's BMW motorcycle with a sidecar, two pick-up trucks, the Lake Detective's Tahoe, and Darlene's bicycle with the sails down. Darlene was just scurrying out when Mr. U arrived.

"Needed more dry ice," Darlene said.

"Nice hat," Mr. U said, his voice muffled behind the mask.

"You guys coming over?" Darlene asked.

It was custom to meet later at Darlene's and toast the GLer who gave the kids the best garage experience. Early reports favored Lloyd Jett, who was letting kids take turns standing in the plaster casts of The Creature's paw prints.

"Later," Mr. U said.

Inside, at the counter, the guys were buying more hardware. Pete was beaming. With this much activity he knew that parents would be coming in all the next week to buy the hardware their kids didn't get on Halloween.

A few residents did up a frightful routine, playing what sounded like haunt-ed disco music or tape loops of agonized ghosts and cackling witches, but mostly they were people who hadn't yet paid a visit to Darlene's house.

Darlene did it right. Darlene's Halloween was perfect. Every kid would take from Darlene's house a lasting impression that served them just as usefully as all the hardware they would collect in the alleys.

Darlene's front yard sloped gently for about fifty yards to the street, with a crooked stone walkway way that led to her front porch. Pine trees framed the porch. New kids stood quivering on the street, staring up at the porch, illuminated by one dusty yellow bulb that spilled just enough light to see that a witch was sitting on the porch stirring a black cauldron of brew. Smoke from dry ice swirled up from the pot and wrapped around Darlene's peaked hat.

One yellow light, fifty yards away. A witch, a real *Wizard of Oz* witch, sitting on a cane-backed chair, stirring a black pot.

Slowly, the kids approached the front door. Darlene was softly humming, but something pleasant and lilting. For some reason that made it spookier. A witch should be raspy and threatening.

Closer, the kids squeezed together, daring each other to be the one who said, "Trick or treat."

Darlene pretended not to see them, the pirates, the hobos, the cowboys, the ballerinas, clinging to each other, their eyes wide with fright. Slowly, she turned her head to the door and smiled with blackened teeth, nodding that they should enter.

Oh, what a test of courage! Who would be the first? The three cowboys were weighted down with wheels, nuts, bolts, axels, and washers.

"She's got Junior Mints," one of the cowboys whispered.

"Let's go in," whispered a second cowboy.

Darlene played into their trepidation, giving her ladle a little flick so that more smoke from the dry ice made an apparition of fog goblins on the porch.

"I don't like Junior Mints," the third cowboy said.

"Chicken," the other two said.

Finally, they summoned the courage to open the door. Two cowboys stepped through. They were only inches away from Darlene.

"All of you," Darlene whispered.

The third cowboy, wincing, squeezed through the door, as if opening the door all the way would expose him to unimaginable horrors.

"Ah, that's better," Darlene said, stirring the pot so that smoke swirled about her face.

"Trick . . . trick or treat," they stammered.

"Give me a shot or two," Darlene said.

They looked at each other dumbfounded. The cowboys pulled out their cap guns and fired, blew smoke from the barrels, and reholstered,

"You know what caps are, don't you?" Darlene asked.

"Bebebebebbbbegggginner fireworks."

"Very good, cowboys, very good. Now take some candy and leave me with my brew."

She started humming sweetly again as the cowboys raced down the yard to the safety of the street.

Two pirates and a Cinderella were waiting.

"What's she got?" the kids asked.

"Junior Mints," the cowboys said, running, hardware jangling in their sacks.

Garage Wood

1. Substantial blocks of abused wood of unknown origin that remain with you throughout your life. They get kicked under a workbench or into a corner when not needed to support a transmission, chock trailer wheels, or test drill bits. You cannot purchase such wood; it is priceless. You might think you don't need it, but you will.
2. Wood with a long history. Why else would you call a child "a chip off the old block?"

Nobody necessarily knows where the special block comes from. It gets retrieved from a construction site dumpster, maybe, or it gets discovered in a pile of split firewood up at the cabin, or an old granary got torn down in town and people migrated to the site and hauled away grain-scoured blocks of timber, as good as taking nuggets of gold from a stream.

It is wood with its own mystery.

Even if it is known where it comes from, it is not known why that particular piece of wood, of all the pieces of wood in the world, got so perfectly assigned to the role it plays in garage life. Blocks of wood are as important as any tool in the chest.

For most applications the garage wood is a block, dented, chipped, beat up. But for some it is a plank or a collection of different-sized scraps from which a correct piece is chosen for a particular task.

Garage wood cannot be purchased. If it was purchased it might get taken care of, or more might be expected of it. In only the rarest circumstances can garage wood be given as a gift to a blockless friend or neighbor.

The wood finds the person and then sticks around without any expectations, like John Wayne's antisocial dog, Sam, in *Hondo*. Wayne didn't feed it, and he didn't give it any water. He loved Sam, but he didn't want the dog to get any ideas.

Farrington's Garage Wood

"Here he comes," the mayor said. "Two Cycle is right behind him."

Galen Farrington picked his way down the shoreline of Spoon Lake, head down, scrambling along over the rocks. He toted a worn canvas sack over his shoulder. When he saw something he liked he bent and picked it up and dropped it into the canvas sack, a few rocks, but mostly wood pieces, bits of driftwood or chunks of dock planks.

"Galen must smell this stuff," the Lake Detective said.

The mayor, LD, and Mr. Unbelievable were tearing apart an old wood boat hoist that had been stacked on the Lake Detective's property for fifty years. LD had photos in the family album that showed the hoist holding a Garwood speedboat. In the pictures, the big framework, stringers, and bracing timbers looked like some kind of medieval catapult.

LD had a modern aluminum dock that went out in sections, and he kept his work skiff on a ShoreStation. LD's wife fancied potted plants and Adirondack chairs on the beach. She called the boat hoist pile "old muskrat wood," and she wanted it gone.

Closer now, Farrington pretended that he wasn't paying any attention. The crew knew better. Farrington was scavenging for wood.

"Hello, Galen," the mayor said.

Farrington nodded. He set his bag down and lit a cigarette. Nobody in Garage Logic knew Galen that well. He kept to himself, but he always seemed to be followed around by Two Cycle, the town dog. He probably had the lowest cylinder index in town: four. A measly four. He parked his old sun-faded Honda Civic, the sum total of his spark plugs, in his driveway. He cut his grass with a push lawn mower that made a clickety-clack sound. He hired neighborhood kids to shovel his snow and clear storm debris. When he went fishing he rented a boat from Germain's Rentals on Spoon Lake and rowed.

Rowed!

Galen finished his cigarette and pinched off the glowing tip before he put the stub in the pocket of his jacket.

"Gonna burn it, LD?" Galen said, studying the pile that had been sawn and tossed together.

"Take what you want, Galen," LD said. "I'll burn what's left."

They had seen Galen show up at job sites and farm auctions. Around town he was always peeking into dumpsters or poking around behind the high school's shop class, looking for wood scraps.

When the Garage Logic Granary was torn down, Galen loaded his little Civic with four scoured timbers that weighed the car down so much the rear bumper scraped the pavement as he drove home.

The crew resumed cutting and piling the boat hoist debris into the makings of a bonfire. Farrington crabbed around the edges of the pile, examining blocks of weathered wood, accepting some, rejecting others. Some of the chunks he held in two hands and turned over and over, like he was examining a rare jewel or something he hadn't seen before. On a couple of pieces he sought the dog's approval.

"There's some beautiful stuff here," Galen said. "You don't need it?"

"Got plenty of garage wood, Galen," LD said.

"What do you do with it?" Galen asked.

It was an odd question. Nothing was done with garage wood. It was just there, to chock trailer tires or test drill bits or shim a lazy workbench leg.

"I don't know, Galen," LD said. "It just seems that when I need a block I've got one."

"Always useful in some unexpected way," the mayor said.

"I've got engines on old blocks," Mr. U said.

Farrington lit another cigarette and stared out at the water.

"What do you do with it, Galen?" They figured him for sixty, maybe seventy, hard to tell. He wasn't married. His long, coal-colored hair was drawn back in a ponytail. He was reed-thin, one of those tough, wiry guys. His face was deeply lined and had a nicotine stain below his right eye.

"You're sure, now?" Galen said, hefting another cut block.

"It's okay," LD said.

Farrington selected a few more pieces and tossed them into his bag. He slung the bag over his shoulder, stooped a little under the new weight, and walked back down the shoreline the way he came, Two Cycle lollygagging behind.

"How did he know we were cutting wood?" LD said.

"He always knows," the mayor said.

Doc Spursm was having a beer at the Knack when he saw the mayor on the hardware floor and waved him over.

"Old Farrington came in to see me," Doc said. "I'm not supposed to talk about things like this, but old Farrington doesn't have long."

"Aw, man, that's not good." It hit the mayor hard, instantly, like Galen, who he really didn't know, was somebody he had known forever.

"When's the last time you ran into him?" Doc said.

The mayor thought for a moment. Then it came to him.

"Last fall," the mayor said. "We were cutting up LD's old boat hoist, and Galen showed up to collect some of the pieces."

"He hasn't been up to speed lately," Doc said.

"He's only about sixty, right, seventy at the most?"

"Mayor," Doc said, "Galen is eighty-three years old."

"Come on."

"I'm not kidding. He's eighty-three, be eighty-four next month. It wasn't like him to even tell me that, a birthday coming up. I had his birth date on my chart, but he told me. Wasn't like him at all."

"What's he been doing for money all these years, Doc?"

Doc took a sip of beer and shot the mayor a sideways glance.

"You don't know? You honestly don't know?"

The mayor felt suddenly shirking of his duty. To most people in Garage Logic, Galen was just a guy around town. He showed up from time to time at the Christmas concert, Last Drop Days, or the fireworks shows, but he didn't hang around the Knack that much, and nobody ever saw him at St. Mclaren's. The only time anybody ever saw Galen for certain was when there was some wood to be had.

"He's had his own gallery in New York for the last thirty years," Doc said.

"What the hell are you talking about, Doc?"

"His own gallery," Doc said. "The Farrington Art Gallery."

"His own art gallery?" the CP asked. "Galen?"

"Yes, Galen, our Galen, the town's Galen."

"Wow."

"I'll be damned!" the mayor said, slamming his hand on the kitchen table, "that explains it."

"What?"

"The trucks," the mayor said. "UPS trucks. It never occurred to me why a UPS truck would be stopping at Galen's. I didn't pay any attention."

It danced around the edge of the mayor's curiosity: four, five times a year, those big, boxy UPS trucks parked in Farrington's driveway.

"We should throw a party for him," the CP said. "He told Doc his birthday was coming up. If Doc figured that was strange behavior for Galen, then maybe he wanted some people around."

But they didn't have to plan anything. The invitation to Galen Farrington's eighty-fourth birthday celebration arrived in the mail two days later, calligraphy on expensive, creamy paper stock. Everybody the mayor talked to received the same invitation:

Farrington's garage, 7 p.m., Sept. 24

Nobody knew what to expect. Farrington's garage door was never open. Nobody had ever been inside. On the night of the twenty-fourth, dozens of people gathered in Farrington's driveway, people from in town and people from out in the countryside. Even Two Cycle was there, sitting patiently by the closed door. At seven p.m. the garage door opened. Farrington stood there in a silky black sport coat, crisp white shirt open at the collar. He wore pressed, gray slacks and tasseled Cole Hahn loafers. His hair was cut. He was smoking a cigarette. He didn't look like Farrington. He looked like an old rock star. He looked like an artist.

"Come on in," he said, lifting his glass of champagne.

It wasn't a garage. It was a woodworking shop, a studio, the likes of which nobody in town had ever seen—clean, aromatic of wood and tools, of oils and varnishes, stains and paints. There were four workbenches, each illuminated by the soft glow from Mission lamps. The floor was spotless, concrete polished to the sheen and hardness of granite. Framed photographs of long-gone boathouses on Spoon Lake adorned the walls. One workbench was devoted entirely to busts carved from blocks of wood: Churchill, Lincoln, Teddy Roosevelt, Bob Dylan. Busts created from blocks of ancient wood, boat-hoist wood, granary wood, wood that captured craggy cheeks, bony chins and deep-set eyes.

"Sweet mother of Jesus," the mayor whispered.

"Champagne?"

She stood in front of the mayor with a dozen glasses of champagne on a tray. The mayor took one. The CP took one. The server said her name was Lilly. She moved gracefully through the crowd.

The variety of wood was amazing: planks, boards, dowels, blocks, a box of mahogany scraps marked "too small to throw away." Farrington even had the old wooden tee markers from Creature Path Golf Course, round wood balls with "Creature Path" wood-burned into the surfaces.

The birthday guests were drawn everywhere in the garage, their senses alive. Their eyes were on carved blocks of wood that were unmistakably moons, half moons, slivers of moons, round moons, goodnight moons, all apparently created with a draw knife over and around and through beat-up blocks of wood that Farrington had salvaged over the years.

Moons hung from the rafters. Freestanding moons perched atop stands. Bookshelf moons were tucked onto shelves.

"Let me show you," Farrington said.

He dimmed the lights in the studio until only one small beam from a track shone on a half moon impaled on a piece of what looked like stainless steel plumbing pipe. The base was a wood block. The half moon mimicked the ancient, distant, gray patina of the moon. The dents and cracks in the wood looked like canyons and a splash of blood-red mahogany stain told of a sailor's warning.

Incredible.

"That came from your old boat hoist, LD," Farrington said, "that day I was out there picking. I want you to have it."

"It's fantastic," LD said.

A canvas, like a stage curtain, covered the back of the studio. Farrington led his guests to the edge of the canvas.

"Lilly," Galen said, "would you do us the honor?"

Lilly put down her tray of champagne and gave Galen a squeeze on his arm.

"Lilly works for me in New York," Galen said.

The canvas was attached by rope and pulleys to a beam in the rafters. As Lilly slowly lifted the canvas, a light automatically turned on and illuminated dozens of wood signs: signs in racks, signs that advertised things like "Apples for Sale," "Black Corn," "Live Bait and Tackle," "Fresh Eggs."

"Go Kart Track," read another. "Amusement Park," "South Shore Resorts," each sign like a missing snippet of film suddenly spliced back onto the reel.

"That's my sign," a fellow in the rear of the garage said, pointing to an ancient road sign hand-painted with lettering that drooled to the bottom of the plank. It said "Fresh Eggs." The lettering was faded, and chips of paint were missing in some of the letters.

"It disappeared one day, about two years ago," the guest said.

"Hey," said another voice, "my uncle had the Go Kart Track."

"We grew black corn."

"I recognize that apple sign."

"Germain's sold live bait and tackle."

Farrington smiled. He wandered into the crowd and stood in front of Bert Williams, a farmer from the outskirts of Garage Logic.

"Bert, I'm sorry about that sudden disappearance," Galen said. "I just had to rescue it. It was perfect when I took it. One more day outside would have been too much. It was just perfect and needed to be saved."

"I don't understand," Williams said.

"The wood had reached a perfect barn gray," Farrington said. "The letters in 'fresh' and 'eggs' were chipped and faded in ways that only nature can accomplish."

"Just an old board," Williams said.

"I have something for you," Farrington said.

Farrington slipped a card from the inside pocket of his sport coat and handed it to Williams. Williams studied the card, which provided a name, Harrison Fallows, a telephone number, and a street address in the Hamptons on Long Island.

"Call that number," Farrington said, "and tell Fallows that you own the sign he has been asking about and offer to sell it to him."

"Sell it?"

"Yes, sell it to him," Farrington said. "It's already been arranged. I've sent him photos of the sign. Sell it."

"Yeah, right," Williams said.

"For thirty thousand dollars," Farrington said. "He's already offered me twenty-five thousand."

Williams clutched his wife's arm. He started to speak but took a gulp of champagne instead. It was a hand-painted sign, a beat-up, weathered plank that said "Fresh Eggs," some kind of drab green color, like old porch floor paint.

"I have cards for all of you," Farrington said.

If the guests didn't get a card from one of Farrington's prospective buyers, they received a moon, a carved moon.

"Lloyd?" Farrington said. Lloyd Jett had been off to the side, keeping to himself.

"Yup, hmm, hmm."

"These are for you, Lloyd," Galen said. He gave Jett two tee markers from Creature Path.

"No. 10," Jett said, looking up, blinking. "I'd…I'd heard the rumors…"

The globes from No. 10 were clawed.

"Golf spikes couldn't do that," Galen said.

"No, sir," Lloyd Jett said. And then. "Thank you, Galen."

"Are you getting it back, Lloyd?" Galen said.

Jett looked up from the clawed globes. "I believe I am, Galen, I believe I am."

Holton stared at his scarred wooden moon and smiled.

Farrington, beaming now and raising his glass to Jett and to all of them, was having a birthday party in reverse.

Six months later, the town buried Galen Farrington in a casket Farrington had made from wood that he had set aside, wood from all over town and out in the countryside, too.

Going In

1. The act or process of involving the garage, all principal equipment, and as many tools as possible, no matter how simple the chore or benign the request for repair from another member of the household, usually a wife.
2. To complicate, some say needlessly.

    See also: RMVT (Real Mechanical Value of Time) and CITP (Cylinder Index Tasking Priority).

Flashlight, Check.
Toolbelt, Check.
Attitude, Check
He's Going In.

The Glue That Binds

During the week between Christmas and New Year's the mayor was asked to fix a child's chair. One of the legs was loose.

"Fix that chair, will you?" the CP asked.

Since she had her hands full trying to get the Christmas tree outside, he said, "Sure, I'll take it to the garage."

"There's glue in the cabinet above the wine glasses."

He put his boating magazine down and got up and looked.

"Wrong glue," he said. "For a project like this you need wood glue. I might even mix some epoxy."

"Project?" she asked, almost out the door, placing one tentative foot on an icy patch. "You don't have to complicate it."

"Whoa, be careful!" he said. She had started to topple under the weight of the tree but regained her balance just in time.

"It's not complicated to mix two-part epoxy."

"That's not what I mean and you know it," she said, shooting him a look.

She was referring to an infamous intramural episode when he crawled under the sink in an upstairs bathroom to investigate a sudden drop in hot-water pressure. He didn't solve the pressure problem—above his pay grade—but while he was under there he thought it would be a good time to drill a hole in the countertop to snake out of sight an electrical cord for a decorative lamp. One thing led to another, and he had to admit he got going pretty enthusiastically with a jigsaw. He tumbled through the opening he inadvertently cut into the wall of the house and landed on his back in the shrubs near where the CP was having iced tea with one of her friends with whom she discusses floral arrangements.

The mayor once used gasoline to try to melt the hump left by the plow at the end of the driveway. That worked about as well as climbing onto the roof with the leaf blower to try and blow away a dumping of heavy, wet snow.

A man has to do what a man has to do, especially in the glacially moving hours between Christmas and New Year's. Besides, the mayor's CP paints a room white dressed all in black, just to show off. She thinks chair repair should be a snap, when, truthfully, all men know a garage opportunity when they see one.

He knew for starters that the old glue would need to be removed, and that called for more than a dull butter knife or a nail file. Those are kitchen gadgets and beneath the men of the garage. He took the little chair to the garage and turned on the TV, flipping to one of lesser bowl games not named after a fruit or famous snack chip. He got the heat going. Then he dug out a couple of sawhorses and placed the chair upside down on the sawhorses.

He set up the adjustable halogen work lights, bathing the patient in a theatrical glow. The leg, he noted after careful examination, was loose at the seat rail and at one end of the stretcher, as loose as a tooth. Why, in fact, he used a dental pick to poke at the thing. He tugged at the leg.

And broke one of the stretchers, the pieces that run between the legs, connecting them to each other.

But the break was so clean it looked like a manufactured scarf.

The stretcher was still solidly glued into the good side of the chair. That called for the heat gun. He blackened the wood a bit, but you would never see that unless you woke up on the floor under the chair. The heat gun did the trick, and now he had the two pieces of broken stretcher.

Easy.

He mixed some marine-grade epoxy, slathered it along the break, and secured it with two C clamps, only one of which stuck to his hand. He walked over to the chemical shelves, settled on acetone, and with his free hand drizzled the solvent on his stuck hand, freeing it in no time.

One team or the other scored a touchdown and, in celebration, he cracked a beer.

As the epoxy set on the stretcher he checked the leg again and decided the best way to get rid of the old glue would also be the fastest. He used the wire brush on the bench grinder, bringing him back to raw, glue-free wood in about two seconds.

To clean the hole in the seat rail he needed a round file. He didn't have one.

"I have to go to the Knack," he announced back in the house.

"What's that smell?"

"Acetone."

Irresistible temptations arise during spontaneous trips to the hardware store. Basically, projects are how you get tools. Anything else is the temptation part. The mayor ran into the guys at the Knack, and he told them he was going in. He told them he had the same bowl game on back in the garage.

"What bowl game is this anyway?" he asked them.

"The Sealy Posturepedic Box Spring Mattress Bowl," somebody at the end of the bar said.

He got out with the round file, a bottle of wood glue, the industrial-strength contractor clean-up bags, a mop, and a new dental pick, and extra-long tweezers that were on special at the cash register.

Back in the garage he cleaned the hole in the seat rail and fired up the air compressor to blow all the surfaces clean. The air pressure blew the curing stretcher off the workbench onto the floor, springing the clamps. He reset them.

Even with newly purchased glue he favored the epoxy; he made some more and fit the leg into the rail with a gob of the stuff. He would fit the stretcher later. He didn't like the leg just standing there. He remembered his big bar clamps out back in the shed.

As he walked though the kitchen he heard a voice trailing after him.

"Is the chair done?"

"Almost."

"Are you going in?"

"Not at all. I just have to go out to the shed for a minute."

It required moving several outdoor items, including two large table umbrellas, to get to the clamps. He also had to push aside a Swedish pruning saw and suffered a uniform jagged cut on his right hand. Happens all the time with those saws, but they are good saws. One of the umbrellas opened on top of him, and he was suddenly and anxiously in the dark, entwined in the metal spines. He needed help. He could see light spilling onto the floor at the open shed door, and he did a shuffle maneuver to get through the door and back to a kitchen window. He couldn't really blame the CP for shrieking. An umbrella with legs had appeared.

"Help!"

"Oh, for God's sake."

She got one arm free, and then he could snake his other arm out without ruining the delicate metal spines.

"No problem," he said. He folded the umbrella, took it to the shed, found his bar clamps, and returned to the garage through the kitchen.

"Now what?"

"Nothing. I just needed these clamps."

A near-death by umbrella was good for another beer, and he watched the TV for a couple of minutes as a Tech or an A&M scored a touchdown. The stadium was not full. The cheerleaders wore windbreakers. It was raining.

The bar clamps expand to four or five feet. He placed one end on the arm of the chair and drew the clamp out long enough to capture the bottom of the leg he was repairing. Weight proportion was better served by turning the chair on its side so that now, if seen from the mouth of the garage, the chair appeared to have been hurled inside as though in anger and become impaled on a metal bar.

The mayor surveyed his task and, other than tangled extension cords, drops of epoxy, blown sawdust, and open tool drawers, he thought everything was well in hand.

He returned to the garage around ten a.m. the next morning with the nagging feeling that maybe he should have left the heat on in the back room at maybe fifty degrees or so. His suspicion was confirmed when he loosened all the clamps and went to reattach the stretcher. The stretcher held, but because he had to pull the leg out a bit to accommodate the slender lathed end of the stretcher the leg snapped off at the rail.

The epoxy didn't so much cure as freeze.

He went into the house.

"Where do you buy those little chairs?"

"You destroyed that one, didn't you?"

"I most certainly did not. I can fix it. I just thought a new chair would be nice, you know, for the kids."

"That's actually kind of pathetic. That's your story, huh?"

"Not all of it. I bought you some proper wood glue if this ever happens again. It's in the cabinet above the wine glasses."

Going In: Subsets

RMVT—The Real Mechanical Value of Time is similar to Going In but is taken into consideration on only small, preordained tasks, such as putting on the new license plate tabs. Everybody knows this doesn't take long, but it should take long enough to produce a meaningful garage experience, possibly including beer and a ballgame. If asked, you can always say that the plate needed to be removed from the car and straightened from that time it got crunched at the mall.

CITP—Cylinder Index Tasking Priority simply refers to using as many cylinders as possible on a project. For example, a one-cylinder chain saw is adequate to remove a large, storm-damaged tree limb. But why go with one cylinder when you could just as easily use four? Involve a couple of lawn tractors with a rope tied to the broken limb and maybe a sentry in the old Harley Davidson golf cart down on the bend of the street to warn traffic that, any minute now, a couple of lawn tractors will be towing a big tree limb away from a damaged tree, and you have exercised a textbook case of CITP.

The Fourth Garage

We did what any young married couple does when they don't have any money. We knocked out a kitchen wall, built a family room off the back of the house, and expanded the one-car garage into a two-car garage. The budget was so close to the bone that the builder, ingeniously, kept half the old garage and added the new bay under a roof that was longer than the old side, so that it had an odd, off-kilter look. Today architects probably do that on purpose.

The garage was on the alley, the big, now double door south-facing. The first year we lived in the house I was introduced to the idea of the Alley Captain. The Alley Captain was the neighbor whose turn it was to go to each house on either side of the alley each fall to collect the snow-plowing money. I quickly entered into the spirit of the captaincy when it was my turn. I thought about wearing a uniform, something on the order of the surgeon general. At some stops it was an occasion for a garage cocktail.

There is no better way to know your neighbors than to serve a year as the Alley Captain. It definitely is the captain's fault if the alley is not plowed in time or plowed poorly. Some of the city alleys were impossibly narrow and crowned—ours was one of them—and expert plowing was critical to winter survival. God help the captain when the plow jockey didn't show up at all.

If a neighbor was particularly accusatory I requested that I be called "Captain."

"It's your fault," one guy told me. "You hired the guy. The guy is a bum, and let me tell you something else, pal..."

He was contending that the plow blade had chipped a bit of the concrete foundation on his garage.

"Make that *Captain*," I said. "That's *Captain* to you."

"Excuse me?"

"I'm serving in an official capacity here. You will please refer to me as *Captain*."

That could get a door slammed in your face.

Heeding a genetic predisposition, boats were brought to this garage in the middle of the city, ancient mahogany Chris Crafts in such utter disrepair that the neighbors eyed me suspiciously through a crack in their blinds or from half-open doors. A couple of those boats were so boxy and blackened from time that they looked liked caskets.

The garage was only eighteen feet deep, if that. I had to punch a hole in the garage wall to accommodate the tongue of the trailer under one of the boats. When the CP stood in the family room and surveyed her tiny estate she could see a trailer tongue sticking through the hole in the wall. Probably shouldn't have done that. It caused intramural strife, a domestic stir, something about my careless acceptance of proprietorship.

We turned boats over in the alley. It required ten or twelve guys. The boats weighed fifteen hundred pounds. On a turning day the mothers would gather children close and stand back, believing the task to be so monumentally dangerous that they envisioned total collapse, a boat teetering in the air and then falling on us, like the house on the Wicked Witch.

After a successful flip, we humped the boat into the garage upside down so the bottom could be repaired. The kids got into this. You could give a little kid a long flat piece of wood and an electric sander and the kid was good for an hour or more.

Kids kept coming. And bicycles, sports equipment, Donald Duck wading pools, lawn furniture. The Cylinder Index climbed. Had to have two cars.

One day the CP came out to the garage and leaned her hip on the door and said, "You either find us a bigger place or you're out."

She was kidding.

I think.

We did what any slightly older married couple would do when they don't have any money. We found a bigger place.

48-Hour Rule

1. After the purchase of something—anything—that might be easily enough noticed in the garage in the routines of daily life, the purchaser has to account for the acquisition only if it is noticed in the first forty-eight hours after its arrival. If, on the forty-ninth hour and thereafter, the item is noticed and the purchaser confronted, the purchaser is entitled to respond with, "That old thing? That's been here forever."

   Note: Works best with acquisitions of items of a kind: motorcycles, for example, or outboard motors.

   See: Three Prices You Pay.

But isn't there a bit of an ethical twinge, one might wonder, in arbitrarily assigning only two days to the waiting period before you are off the hook? Go ahead and make it seventy-two hours if you wish, or two months. Garage Logicians stick with forty-eight hours and have concluded that there is virtually a national consensus on the time. The 48-hour rule is not only useful, but it cuts to the very heart of the domestic relationship. How well one or the other of you is actually paying attention is unfailingly told in this rule.

There are a couple of things to remember to use the rule in good faith. The definition suggests an item "easily enough noticed." The rule cannot possibly apply to screwdrivers or cans of paint or even a new battery-operated drill. Those items are procured on an ongoing basis and are needed for daily tasks.

The rule really only comes into play on items of significance, which implies it getting noticed, and, relative to the price of a drill, a cost that would be considered out of the ordinary.

In other words, use the 48-hour rule when you know you are in trouble for hauling it home.

There. Let it be noted. This is the sneaking something past her rule, or his, motorcycles, lawn mowers, snowblowers, shotguns. In the news recently was a guy in Wisconsin who stole a tank and parked it in his driveway. Garage Logicians thought that if that guy got away with the 48-hour rule it might weigh in his favor in court.

Ah, but in good faith remember the implied obligation of the other to be paying attention. The acquisition cannot be hidden for forty-eight hours. And the bigger the item, the more carefully measures must be taken to store it, place it, park it or display it in a normal manner. Another outboard motor cannot be hauled home and disguised behind push brooms and bicycles and cardboard boxes. Nothing can be draped over it. It's just there. And if it doesn't get noticed in forty-eight hours, all garage acquisition obligations have been fulfilled.

Acquisition

The mayor tromped through deep snow to Mr. Unbelievable's garage, carrying the Sunday classified ads from the *Liberal Lakes Herald*. This was years ago, so long ago that newspapers still had great big fat Sunday classified ad sections, Sunday papers so heavy you could hear them tossed on a porch from a block away.

In this particular edition of the *Herald* a 1966 Honda Benly 150 motorcycle was advertised, one of Honda's elegant period pieces of the square headlight and swooping fenders era. Those bikes are sometimes incorrectly referred to as Dreams. Mr. Unbelievable, for example, had a 1965 Honda 305 Dream. The Benly has a smaller displacement than a Dream, an important garage distinction.

"We've got to call this guy," the mayor said, waving the paper.

Mr. U was storing seven of his best motorcycles indoors during the winter, in the family room immediately inside the garage service door. But he felt a change coming, sometimes manifested by a tingling along his spine whenever he was near the bikes, as though Mrs. U was shooting him looks from a different part of the house. He was afraid his long, lucky run of indoor storage was coming to an end.

"Come on, man," he said, "one more bike in here could upset the delicate balance, get me kicked out of the inside room."

"You've got two bikes present," the mayor said, "one large snowblower, and three antique snowmobiles. She wouldn't notice."

"What about you?"

"Obviously it would get noticed. I don't even have a bike yet. You are definitely the best bet."

"I'm low on cash," Mr. U said.

"I'll be the banker," the mayor said.

These transactions can get complicated. They hadn't even called the guy yet.

"Get a phone."

Mr. U got a phone, dialed the number, and handed the phone to the mayor. The mayor got the information and, glancing at Mr. U, said they would be over. Mr. U nodded.

"How much?" he asked, after the hang-up.

"The guy said eight hundred dollars."

"That's not bad, if it's all there," Mr. U said.

In any acquisition, "it's all there" is a code term for originality, that the item is fairly intact, with original parts. It gets disappointing to chase down, say, an advertised 1930 Model A Ford only to discover it has a Plymouth hood, Cadillac rear wheels, and an interior from an AMC Gremlin.

During a two-year stretch after the release of the movie *On Golden Pond*, the mayor made at least fifty acquisition runs to see boats advertised as "just like *On Golden Pond*." In the movie, Henry Fonda's boat was a twenty-two-foot Chris Craft Sportsman. They were manufactured between 1946 and 1954. Not once in those fifty runs did he see a Sportsman. He saw aluminum boats, fiberglass boats, and, strangest of all, a yellow-and-black, homemade, twelve-foot plywood boat that looked like a bumblebee.

The mayor went home to tell the CP that he had to help Mr. Unbelievable make a run to Liberal Lakes to possibly acquire a motorcycle.

"Not another one?"

"Well..."

Mr. Unbelievable, meanwhile, went inside to tell his CP that he was going to use his trailer to help the mayor possibly bring home a motorcycle that they had found in that day's newspaper. Those weren't really lies. The boys were merely laying down a fallback foundation.

They hooked up Mr. U's beat-up snowmobile trailer to Mr. U's Lincoln and set off for Liberal Lakes around noon. An acquisition run builds its own vibe. The imagination runs wild with possibility. The moment of discovery draws near with a quickening of the imaginative heart. Maybe even a quickening of the romantic heart. The discovery runs are at least as enjoyable as actual possession. It's the hunt that gets remembered around the garage heater on cold winter nights.

"You've got the pin in, right?"

"The pin is in," Mr. U said, ashing his cigarette out the cracked vent window. "Don't be such a self-preservationist."

"Not wanting to die violently has nothing to do with self-preservation."

"The pin is in."

The J-Pin secures the hitch to the receiver. The previous summer, Mr. U had left the hitch in the receiver, violating a fundamental rule of nature. You can free the J-Pin, no problem, but hitches left in receivers tend to rust in place. Mr. U tried everything—pry bar, hammer, his angry bootheel. That hitch was welded tight to the Lincoln. He even tried using one of the mayor's cable hoists to pull the hitch out after soaking it for twenty-four hours in WD-40. They hooked one end of the cable around the ball on the hitch and ran the cable back to hook it around a maple tree. Mr. U put the Lincoln in drive and then, when the cable was taut, accelerated in short bursts.

"Anything?" he asked, craning out the window.

As a kid the mayor was once knocked out cold, cranking a boat out of the water. The metal crank handle on the hoist fractured and banged off his head, knocking him fifteen feet from the dock and into shallow water face-down, like he was doing a dead man's float. He was retrieved by his father. He was seeing birdies that day, and he'd been shy of hoists and ratchets and taut cable ever since.

The mayor leaned in for a closer look.

"Nothing," he said, backing away quickly.

Mr. U tried again. Still nothing. Again. Nothing. And then, a distinct crack.

"Anything now?"

"I'll say."

"What?"

"You killed the tree."

They abandoned the project, and the mayor had forgotten about it until one day in the fall, when they got a call to fetch a free motorcycle if they wanted it, an old Honda 550. Of course they wanted it. They didn't pass up free cylinders. Off they went on about a twenty-mile search for an address in Diversityville, found it, loaded the bike (not bad, all there) onto the snowmobile trailer and headed back to Garage Logic.

Still on surface streets, they came to a stop sign and were suddenly slammed into from behind.

"What the hell...?"

"All right!" Mr. U said, bounding cheerfully from the car.

The mayor could not believe what his friend had done. He had hauled the trailer those twenty miles without the J-Pin securing the hitch to the receiver and was apparently willing to keep trailering without it, hoping for exactly what happened. The constant vibrating and jarring of the trailer broke the bonds of rust and freed the hitch from the receiver.

"Are you nuts!" the mayor shouted. "That could have happened on the freeway."

Mr. U lit a cigarette.

"We aren't on the freeway. It worked, didn't it?"

"Jesus, Mary, and Joseph."

"Besides, the safety chains are hooked up."

"Eight hundred bucks isn't bad," Mr. U said.

"There's something else working in our favor," the mayor said, "the guy said he's a big Green Bay Packers fan, and he wasn't even going to answer the phone past noon."

"Why?"

Mr. U is not a sports fan. The mayor cannot account for that shortcoming, except to understand that when the kids were playing ball up at the high school or shooting pucks on the frozen lake, Mr. U was taking apart minibikes in his parents' living room.

"Today is the Super Bowl, pal, the Holy Grail."

"Isn't Green Bay always in it?"

The mayor sighed.

"Not since the first two, 1967 and 1968."

Mr. U compliments the mayor on these occasions for what he believes to be the mayor's encyclopedic knowledge of sports. The mayor's mother might have known that Green Bay was in the first two, certainly the first ever.

"He'll want this thing done and out of his life," the mayor said.

"Where do we put it?"

"We'll think of something."

"It would go nicely," Mr. U said, "with my 305 Dream."

That was the spirit. The mayor needed his buddy thinking in acquisition terms. The mayor had an idea percolating about where they could put the bike.

They found the address easily enough. Not many houses in Liberal Lakes featured a large cardboard Green Bay helmet propped in the snow in the front yard and green and gold tinsel laced in the front windows like Christmas decorations.

"This has to be it," Mr. U said.

"You think?"

They turned around at the end of the block and came up on Green Bay's side of the street.

"You're the buyer," Mr. U said. "I'm the critic."

"Check."

They knocked on the front door, and the fellow answered quickly. The bike was behind him on the porch. The initial glance said it was all there, including what were probably the original whitewall tires. The mayor's eye caught the inside of the house, a phantasmagoria of Green Bay kitsch, including a life-size color cardboard cutout of Paul Hornung in his No. 5 uniform, his arm outstretched to break a tackle.

"What do you need for it?" the mayor asked, scratching his head, but mostly at Paul Hornung.

"I'm asking eight hundred dollars."

Oh, those magic words. By letting it slip that he was "asking," he was also listening. A woman was scurrying around inside the house, appearing from what must have been the kitchen to load down the dining room table with chips and cheese and meat. There was a keg, they now noticed, cooling on the porch behind the bike.

"Man, I don't know," Mr. U said, sliding into his role. "The seat is torn; the rear fender has a little crease. I don't know. Does it run?"

"It did," the owner said, studying the license tab, "in 1991."

"That was the last time?" the mayor asked. It was agreed that at some point the mayor would morph from the eager buyer to a more cautious type who would listen to wise counsel.

"Dude," the owner said, "it is what it is."

"I take it you like Green Bay, today," the mayor said.

"You got that right," he said.

"I don't know," Mr. U said, honestly oblivious to football.

"I'll give you three hundred cash," the mayor said.

"You're wasting my time."

"Four hundred."

"I'll wait until spring."

No, he wouldn't. The bike was on the porch. It was ready to be wheeled out the door. No Green Bay fan worth his spinach green and gold colors would advertise a bike on Super Bowl Sunday if he didn't need to get rid of it. The mayor thought he knew the reason why. She kept throwing glances from inside the house and nailed him at least three times with bank-shot

Looks off the mirror above their fireplace in the living room. The guy actually winced when he got hit by one of them.

"Five hundred."

He looked at his watch. He deflected another look, but it grazed him.

"Man, you're close."

Five-fifty is as close as I get," the mayor said.

"Okay, done."

"Let's put it in your shed," the mayor said.

They were heading back to Garage Logic, the bike secured by straps in the trailer. They were coming down off the post-purchase high. Those were the original whitewalls, original blue paint, too.

"We stick it in the shed; let things settle down."

"We could park it in there," he said.

"Damn right," the mayor said, "She never goes out there."

"No…"

Mr. U was still worried about discovery.

"But let's leave it on the trailer and do it tonight," he said.

They pulled into the driveway, and the mayor walked home. If Mr. U was asked if he bought a bike he could honestly answer that he did not. As for the mayor, the usual gang of family and friends had arrived for the Super Bowl and he wasn't asked anything.

At about nine p.m. the mayor announced that he was logy from watching the game and that he was going for a walk. He hustled over to Mr. U's garage, saw a glowing cigarette tip in the dark shadow of the service door, and asked, "Is the coast clear?"

"I guess."

They drove with the lights off a half block around the street to the shed, which sits between their two places. They removed the straps, grunted the bike off the trailer, and stuck it in the shed. They left a couple of narrow tire tracks, but that was it. Wind off the lake would cover the tracks in snow.

The mayor let a few days go by. He checked back midweek. Mr. U said he was itching to explore the bike. So was the mayor.

"I think we should bring it down here," Mr. U said.

"When?"

"Now. The boss is taking a nap."

They went to the shed and rescued the bike from the cold, wheeled it through the snow, and entered the warm garage. They didn't try to hide the tire tracks in the yard. Good-looking bike. It was all Mr. U could do to keep from taking the carburetor off immediately.

They didn't hide the bike or disguise it or obscure it. It seemed to dawn on them simultaneously that they were behaving ethically.

"It's in the garage," Mr. U said, almost to himself. "I mean, if a few days pass and nothing happens...I don't know."

"That's cool with me."

Two days passed. On Friday night the mayor made another appearance.

"She notice it?"

"Nope."

"It's been forty-eight hours," the mayor said.

"I'm home free," Mr. U said. "By the way, watch this."

He gave the starter a gentle kick and it purred to life. Ran nice and quiet.

"You dog!"

It did get noticed, about a week later. When the mayor asked Mr. U what he told the boss, he said he told her that it had been around forever, you know, the blue one. He said she nodded, as though remembering.

"I think we should call it the 48-hour rule," the mayor said.

"Absolutely," Mr. U said.

WD-40

A magic elixir for lubrication that, in addition to its other applications, makes an emergency cologne.

The Lake Detective

Herb Stempley went up in his Piper Cub at about three p.m. on Thursday, January 7, as he does most days about that time, leaving from the Garage Logic Airfield, a bare-bones place, one paved strip, one hangar, one orange windsock.

Stempley has four airplanes, contributing to his impressive Cylinder Index of 324. He liked to fly over the town and especially liked to buzz the high-school football games in the fall, dipping a wing to the Fighting Wrenches.

On this day he flew out over Spoon Lake, could not believe what he was seeing, and circled back. Spoon Lake, 7,200 acres of coves and small islands, with an open body of about 4,000 acres, was ice-clear in the middle. Open! It had been a brutally cold autumn. Spoon Lake iced over on November 30 and by mid-December featured ice about fifteen inches thick. Ice fishermen in town predicted ice two to three feet thick for the winter. On January 7, when Stempley took off, it was two below.

But there was dark, brooding, open water in the middle of the lake.

Stempley returned to the airfield, buttoned up the Piper, and drove straight to the mayor's house. Herb fancied a leather World War I helmet when he flew, and he was still wearing it with his goggles pushed up on his forehead when he knocked on the mayor's door.

"I was just up over the lake, Mayor," Herb said, "and I saw the strangest thing. Open water."

"What?"

"Right in the middle, open water, I'd say a half mile long and a hundred yards wide, maybe wider."

"What?"

"Open water."

"I know. I mean, how? Why? It hasn't been as warm as fifteen degrees since Thanksgiving." He brought Herb in from the cold.

"I'm telling you, open water, and we better get the word out."

Garage Logic had such an active snowmobile population that it was a miracle somebody hadn't already taken the plunge racing across the lake.

"I'll call the *Logician*," the mayor said, "and I'll call the police. Larry will have to get caution lights at the public access."

"Bait stores, too," Herb said. "They can put signs up."

"And we'll need to get the Lake Detective involved," the mayor said. "He'll know what to do."

The Lake Detective lives on a cove on the northwest corner of Spoon Lake in a house that a few of the people in town always imagined had World War II significance. They don't know why, maybe the stone foundation or the remains of an elaborate clothes-pole that resembled a mast with stays. To the imagination it might just as well have been a decommissioned communications tower. Sturdy, set back on a mossy hillock and hidden from the lake in the pines, it had the feel of a place where agents—maybe not even ours was one of the darkest suspicions—might have spread big maps on tables and used radio equipment with dials like the faces of old, yellowed, Bulova wristwatches.

LD never disabused anybody of that notion and rather enjoyed the speculation. To him it was just his house, but he figured it was good for business if the ambience suggested intrigue or dark mysteries, for that is what he was good at. Solving the dark mysteries of lakes and rivers.

"Long, leggy blonde," the mayor said when a woman matching that description opened the door to find the mayor and Stempley standing outside. Her name is Chloe, but she plays along with her husband's detective image. In truth they both hold master's degrees in aquatic biology and civil engineering, but they have had so much fun with the detective angle that they named their business Blue Water Mysteries, even though LD's principal source of income is contract work, weed and algae control. Lake associations and watershed districts hire him, as well as public beach groups and private homeowners.

"What can I do for you boys?" Chloe said.

"Need to see the detective," the mayor said.

"Got a case?" Chloe asked, winking.

"Spoon Lake is open in the middle," Stempley blurted.

"In this weather?" Chloe said.

She lifted an old-style telephone receiver off a hook in the hall and clicked it twice. "Steve, the mayor and Herb are here. Spoon Lake is open in the middle."

They heard him squawk at the other end.

"Go on out," she said, "he's in the boathouse."

They tromped through the snow down to the shore and climbed the steps leading to the second story of the boathouse, which had the same stone foundation as the house. LD had the door cracked for them. A fire snapped and popped in the hearth. He produced the office bottle and set out three shot glasses.

"Only one thing it could be," he said before they could get a word out.

His office was a museum of what he had retrieved off the bottoms of lakes: old eggbeater outboard motors, rusty flashlights, antique beer bottles, anchors, chains, fishing lures and tackle boxes, bow lights and sailboat rudders.

"Cheers," LD said, lifting his glass. "I bet we haven't had a groundwater recharge in thirty years."

"Speak English, LD," Stempley said. LD had a couple of stuffed chairs, and they pulled them close to the fire and sat back and sipped the whisky.

The mayor was already feeling better. He thought maybe something had crashed out there.

"We had intense rain last fall," LD said. "Intense rain in a short period. That water had to go someplace. It finds its way into the old pipes."

"You lost me there, LD," the mayor said.

"Not real pipes," LD said. "I'm talking about subterranean channels, piping, or flow ways. The water kind of pulses along, taking its time. Groundwater is about fifty-five degrees. When it enters the lake it rises to the surface and melts the ice."

"But I flew over the lake last week," Herb said, "and it wasn't open then."

LD took a sip of whisky and tossed another log onto the fire.

"The water squirts along in surges," he said, making a snaking motion with his hand. "The surge stops, no new warm water enters the lake, and the lake freezes over. The pulse starts again, new water enters the lake, and the hole opens up. I bet this is happening on a lot of lakes in the state this winter."

The mayor finally said it. "Man, that's a relief. I thought maybe something crashed out there."

"Focus recharge," LD said, sinking back in his chair. "Not much to be made of that. If you want I can put a few of my flow meters into Two Cycle Creek and run a hydrograph chart."

"Might as well be certain," the mayor said.

"Tell anybody?" LD asked.

"The *Logician*, Larry, couple of bait stores," they said.

"Good enough," LD said. "Keep the snowmobilers away for a while. It'll freeze over solid before winter is done."

The *Associated Press* in Euphoria picked up the original *Logician* story—the one before the addition of the Lake Detective's explanation; that never did get picked up—and called it "Global Warming Blamed for Mystery Hole in Spoon Lake Ice."

The mayor read that story on Sunday in the *Liberal Lakes Star Journal*. On Sunday night MSNBC was reporting that a mysterious jagged hole had opened up the ice of Spoon Lake at Garage Logic in east-central Minnesota.

Herb never mentioned jagged.

"Scientists are not discounting catastrophic climate change as the reason for a mysterious hole in the ice of Spoon Lake near Garage Logic, Minnesota," the female anchor intoned with the solemnity that made you want to run from rising ocean levels and scalded prairies.

"Last Thursday," she continued, "a local pilot, Herbert J. Stempley, reported the hole to local authorities. Stempley said the jagged hole was about two miles long and five hundred yards wide."

"No, he didn't!" the mayor yelled at the TV.

The mayor clicked. By God, they were all covering it. A young guy on CNN was interviewing a Dr. Ewing Singer, of Fairleigh Dickinson University in New Jersey, who was suggesting that a similar hole had appeared on a lake in the Adirondack Mountains in New York in 1987 and that it was thought that the hole on that occasion was caused by a crashed space vehicle.

"This Minnesota phenomenon could quite possibly be a similar extraterrestrial crash," Dr. Ewing said.

"Possibly caused by global warming?" the CNN anchor with the schoolboy-short hair asked.

"Quite likely," Ewing said. "We just don't know the effects our man-made greenhouse gases have on the sophisticated navigational equipment of our space-bound friends."

The mayor clicked again. The Fox anchor was reminding viewers that "Minnesota has had an unusually warm winter…"

"It's twelve freakin' below!" the mayor yelled at the anchor.

Even the CP, who finds herself occasionally falling for the spiel about how fluorescent light bulbs will save the earth, said, "These people are nuts."

By Monday the town was under siege: news helicopters, satellite trucks, television teams. CNN and FOX were in town, along with National Public Radio, the *Washington Post*, *USA Today*, and the *New York Times*.

The foghorn was going crazy, too, which meant that the outsiders had to keep starting their live shots over every time they used a word like *appropriate* or *proactive* or *sustainable*.

The mayor's house had been found by the female CNN anchor, Tawny Riddle, who was dressed in arctic clothing so hastily purchased that tags still dangled from her jacket and from the hood of her parka. The mayor plucked a tag off her collar and handed it to her.

"We need you for a live shot," she said.

"Okay."

"I mean outside, on the beach, near the lake."

"Okay."

"Now, please!" she bleated. He got his coat and hat and walked around to the front of the house. The CP smiled at him through the window, making a "loser" L with her thumb and first finger against her forehead. He smiled back. Riddle positioned him with his back to the lake. Her camera guy set up. He said he was ready.

As she listened to her earpiece her tense face transformed itself into an expression of incredible sincerity.

"Yes, Jay, yes, I'm with the mayor of Garage Logic. Mayor, will you be asking for help to solve the mystery of the open water in the lake behind you?"

"Help..."

"From the government."

"Uh, I don't think we need any help. It's just a groundwater recharge."

"With so many aspects of global climate change that we simply do not understand, you don't think federal funding is required to study this case?"

"I don't think it's a case, really; it's warm groundwater entering the lake and eroding the surface ice. The Lake Detective is running a hydrograph for us... and, and, what is the temperature supposed to be? Ever wonder that?"

"Jay," she said, turning away from the mayor so that she alone looked into the camera, "these simple townsfolk are frightened, and I can't blame them. This is scary."

Nobody heard that because the foghorn went off. The mayor told her that if she would meet him at the Knack Hardware and Lounge at six p.m. he would give her an exclusive about the mystery. She shivered with excitement.

He walked around town and promised the same thing, an exclusive, to FOX, NPR, the *Washington Post, USA Today,* and the *New York Times.*

Then he called the Lake Detective and told him of the plan.

"And bring your diplomas," he told him.

LD did his best, told the newsies that he had degrees and that he had been studying things like focus recharge for years, that it wasn't global warming or an extraterrestrial crash or a monster or the rising price of crude oil, just groundwater surging to the surface. He had a newly minted hydrograph to prove it, a measurement in cubic feet per second of the water flow in Two Cycle Creek.

"Look," LD pleaded with the national press, offering them each a copy of his graph work.

The newsies yawned. Most of them were on cell phones or checking their email on handheld devices. Worse, some of them were twittering. Nobody even asked LD any questions.

"He's never been stumped," the mayor blurted, feeling proprietary. "Ask him anything. Come on, ask him. The guy knows everything there is to know about lakes."

One by one they got up and took over the bar at the Knack.

They all left town the next morning, something about a monster thunderstorm in Texas, strange for this time of year, they were saying.

Space Management

1. The nearly constant effort, mostly but not always limited to winter, to keep all your impervious surfaces as exposed as possible to the mothering warmth of the sun.
2. Finding the driveway edges after each snowfall.

When the snow gets deep, don't forget to practice your space management.

Ruined, You're It!

During one of the great snowstorms between the Halloween Blizzard of 1991 and the present time, the people in Garage Logic, two in particular, embraced a strange new activity involving cylinders: The Ruining of Each Other's Driveways.

It sounds ominous and, to an observer from Liberal Lakes or Euphoria who might stumble upon the scene, it might even look deadly, as it did during the storm in question. That's when the mayor got into it pretty good with Herb Stempley, who lives on the other side of Spoon Lake at the end of a half-mile-long driveway.

Herb and the mayor had been ruining each other's driveways for years, and neither one of them could remember now how it started exactly. They are charter members of the Royal Order of the 21sters, Garage Logicians who celebrate the arrival of spring on Dec. 22 because the days are getting longer, and who lament the arrival of June 21 because the days start to get shorter. They would go to each other's houses after a snowstorm to point out what a fine "spring" day they were having, and invariably they were out snow-blowing. It seemed only natural to encroach on the other fellow's new snow, just to see the agitation develop.

"Hey, get out of here! Knock it off you $%#@(!"

In the early days they did it in front of each other. When the attacks came before sunrise they knew which rat had been out in the wee hours.

The mayor would come out of the house, looking forward to one of life's simplest and greatest pleasures—snow-blowing the virgin driveway, only to discover that somebody had driven up and down, up and down, packing the snow. His only consolation was knowing that Herb was facing the same letdown out at his place.

While other GLers were blowing snow in long graceful fountains of fresh powder, the mayor struggled to maintain control of the machine as it rode lopsided up and down the ruts created by the evil Stempley. But again, the mayor knew that Stempley was muttering and complaining on his side of town.

They called a truce from time to time, but those truces never lasted. And the women in their lives expressed disappointment that it was sophomoric behavior they just couldn't shake. The Look didn't even work on them anymore when came to driveway ruination.

As for the great snow between the Halloween storm and the present time, it was a nor'easter that played out over three days, a Thursday, Friday, and Saturday. The mayor had fresh snow on Thursday. Stempley had fresh snow, too, because the mayor didn't have time to get out there. When the mayor had fresh snow on Friday he briefly wondered why. He took the opportunity to practice some of the best space management of his snow-blowing career, the idea of space management being that you absolutely cannot give up space or, before winter is over, all you will have are two crusty ruts from the street to the garage.

Narrowed and treacherous sidewalks, no bigger than goat tracks, are commonly seen in Euphoria and Liberal Lakes, where snowblowers are not much in fashion. Such casually maintained property in the surrounding towns results in driveways barely cleared enough for low-slung little hybrid cars.

But for the likes of Herb and the mayor, space management is practiced with a robust enthusiasm, as it is yet another reason to hear the sweet
sound of an engine at work.

The mayor had an idea on the second night of the storm, Friday
night—dastardly, he admitted. He parked his pickup truck on the street so
he wouldn't ruin the driveway backing out Saturday morning. That night
he listened to the weather forecast long into the evening. Another eight
inches was expected! He slept for about four hours and got up at three a.m.
and made strong, stocking-feet coffee. He didn't want to wake up the CP
clomping around in his snowmobile boots. Unfortunately, he dropped a big
D-cell Mag flashlight. He might as well have dropped a bowling ball.

"What are you doing down there?"

Uh-oh.

"You better not be going out to Stempley's," she warned.

"I just want to check out the storm before the plows, that's all."

"Herb is still pretty mad at you from the last time."

The last time. The mayor had commandeered a town plow and flattened Stempley's driveway so uniformly that Herb had to use his ice chop-
per for a week just to find pavement.

"I remember. Just going to check the conditions. I am the mayor, you
know."

With a big mug of steamy Joe he trudged through the yard and out to
the street. The plows hadn't been out yet, and the forecast was true. He
needed every bit of the truck's four-wheel drive as he headed out to Stempley's place.

What a wonderland of a morning. The sun wasn't even a hint yet over
the lake, but the mayor could just about make out the yellow glint of light
in the Lake Detective's ice shack. He always stayed out on the lake Friday
nights reading bulletins from the Department of Natural Resources.

Downtown was as quiet and peaceful as an Alpine postcard one minute, but almost invisible the next as a gust blew off the lake. Pine trees
sagged under the weight of the new snow. The wind whipped drifts across
the Sparkplug Gap and Reformed Lawyer's Road.

In the open country out around Doppler Radar Park he could just make out the aviation warning lights on the radio broadcast tower.

As he got closer to Stempley's place he drained the last of his coffee. He didn't need headlights and switched them off. It was three-twenty a.m. The mayor almost hesitated. Stempley had practiced his space management to perfection, and ruination was painfully proportional to the intensity of the storm.

Stempley, it should be noted, was Garage Logic's most inventive snow-blower and had been experimenting recently with an old Simplicity bolted to the front of his 1965 BMW motorcycle sidecar. He had been inducted into Bill Johnson's Mower Museum two winters back for his work with a small, one-cylinder lawn mower engine–powered shovel, which was to be used only on the light stuff.

The mayor didn't know what Stempley would have brought out of the garage for this storm, maybe his 1931 Model A pickup truck with the plow blade, a crowd favorite every year at the Last Drop Days parade of antique cylinders. Even with the wind whipping the snow into long, curvaceous drifts across his driveway there were patches of bare ground, and the mayor knew that Herb had taken it down to pavement probably six hours earlier.

The mayor went in.

Up and down he drove, up and down, cranking the wheel to grind the new snow into the concrete. Stempley's driveway flares at the garage end so that a third car can park there, and he got that wedge flattened. He was at the house end of the driveway when he saw a light flick on upstairs. Then another. A flashlight beam danced from window to window. Stempley was up and moving!

The mayor backed out, invisible to the house halfway to the street. He stole back through the night and didn't turn on his headlights until he got about a mile away.

There was time for him to catch a few hours of sleep before he did his own driveway. And he knew Stempley had such difficult work ahead of him that he was safe from recrimination.

It's what happened next, about eleven a.m. Saturday morning, that resulted in a police call and a crowd of about thirty people, virtually all of whom knew Stempley, but still thought he was trying to kill the mayor with Mrs. Stempley's Oldsmobile.

"Mayor, look out!" He heard a cry from somebody. He looked up just in time to see Stempley crash through the plow hump at the end of the driveway.

Stempley wasn't stopping. The mayor cranked his snowblower's chute so that it was pointed at Stempley's charging 1977 Ninety-Eight Regency. As he advanced, the mayor blew snow directly at him. Blinded, Stempley stopped. The mayor paused. Stempley's hand reached out the open window and cleared the snow from his windshield. The mayor knew what Herb was doing. It was the classic defensive measure. He didn't want to work the wipers with an overload. He drove forward again, and the mayor let him have it with another push forward. He had fresh ammunition, undisturbed snow. But Stempley had chains on the Olds. The mayor's auger bit and threw solid waves at Stempley's windshield.

Stempley backed out to the street and turned on his wipers. The mayor could just make him out now, Herb Stempley in full battle cry.

Herb gunned the Olds for a running start. The mayor parried with another blast of the fresh stuff. Herb kept coming. And coming. He had the mayor on the run. The mayor backed up, pulling the machine behind him. He couldn't fire in retreat, but he knew that Stempley's wipers were wearing down. They stopped.

The mayor quickly advanced, taking advantage of Herb's crippled wipers with another load that made a satisfying *whump* on the glass.

"You broke my wipers," the mayor heard him say. But Stempley's voice was muffled by the whine of the competing engines.

The mayor poured it on. He had him now. Stempley couldn't move.

"You're a buffalo stuck in the mud, Stempley," the mayor said.

The mayor heard a siren in the distance but he didn't stop. His only hope was to bury the car. But Stempley's arm came out again, and he cleared a swipe of snow. His mittened hand caught on the driver's side wiper and it broke off. He shook it loose. The Oldsmobile roared and strained and moved forward. He wasn't gunning it this time. The chains biting, he moved methodically, driving the mayor back, back, back against his closed garage door.

Stempley had won. He was just getting out of car when Officer Larry of the Garage Logic Police Department swung the town's one black-and-white into the ruined driveway and cut the siren. The knot of onlookers crept forward.

"Mayor?"

"Yes, officer."

Larry got closer and stopped.

"Stempley, is that you?"

"Hello, Larry."

Larry turned to face the crowd.

"Who called this in?"

Nobody responded.

"One of you is from Euphoria or Liberal Lakes," Larry said, "and you're more than welcome to visit, and I don't care if you identify yourself because there has been no crime here."

He let the crowd have a chance to respond. The GLers were already wandering home.

"What you just saw here is commonplace, at least between these two," he said, jerking his thumb back at the combatants. "They've been at each other for . . . for how long, boys?"

"I don't know, Larry," the mayor said. "We've been trying to figure that out."

"Well, anyway," Larry said to the crowd, "there's nothing more to see. The mayor's driveway is ruined and five will get you ten that Stempley's got ruined earlier this morning."

"I'll say it did," Stempley muttered. "I had it perfect, too."

"But it looked like a murder attempt." The accuser was female. She wore a complete facemask beneath her rabbit-fur hat.

Stempley and the mayor looked at each other, a look she misunderstood.

"I know what you're thinking," she said. "It's not real fur."
She turned on her heels and walked away.
"You coming in, Herby?"
"I got a little time."
"Larry, you want coffee?"
"I could use a jolt."
The three of them surveyed the ruined driveway.
Stempley asked, "Wouldn't real fur be warmer?"

Finally, the Last Real Garage

As this is written I am a man temporarily without a garage. The house I had to find, the or-else house, came down for what might euphemistically be called extensive remodeling. I will be getting a new garage. I didn't watch when a big CAT front-end loader knocked down the house so that the debris piled onto the garage floor. It was a serviceable, trustworthy garage, and I imagine it was fitting to accumulate the weight of the house on its scarred old floor. They got that pile of debris the next day, and the old garage floor, too.

There are spaces for two cars beneath our leased row house at the closed end of a long subterranean bowel that still smells of new concrete and Sheetrock dust. About twenty-four times a day a Titan air exchanger kicks on at my end of the basement and generates a wind speed of approximately seventy-five miles per hour. Modern building codes compelled the air exchanger. I still haven't figured out if it runs on a timer or somehow electronically senses when one of the little hybrid cars—I have counted three—excuses itself and starts quietly.

It is a garage, I suppose, or is advertised as such in the sales literature, but I know garages and this one is not giving off any vibes. The developer keeps a collector car, a 1966 Chevelle, covered in a tight plastic wrap in an empty stall beneath an unsold unit, but I have not seen the car visited or unwrapped. My new row-house neighbors are either at a point in life where they have downsized and left garages behind in another world or they are just starting out and haven't yet discovered the pleasures in store for them in a real garage.

Shoes are left outside the service doors to each unit, which suggests to me that most residents believe the garage to be a mudroom. A fellow about four units down on the backside has a ruby-red MadRiver canoe upside down on sawhorses. I've stared at it. I've seen a few cross-trainer type bicycles and some children's toys, but nothing that would indicate that anybody ever broke apart a transmission down there or ever would. I might be the only occupant who brought tools. My six-drawer chest on wheels and my air compressor just fit inside the storage room provided for each unit under the stairwell.

All my other garage possessions—my garage life, including drums—had to be put into a warehouse in a distant suburb. I visit my stuff on weekends; divorce must be difficult. I am only checking up on things and not people.

I'm not sure anything has ever spilled in this spanking new basement parking garage mudroom thing, certainly not beer or two-part epoxy or motor oil. The place is immaculate, not only because of the Titan cyclone, but because nobody spends any time down there. It can't get dirty. I'm not suggesting that to be authentic a garage has to be a mess. I'm merely saying that a proper garage needs to at least be lived in and a bit dinged around the edges from when the wire wheel on the bench grinder spits screws against the walls or a splattering of mahogany filler stain is dribbled on a cabinet door from the last boat project.

It's a nice place, the row house, new, all the modern amenities. But don't these people argue? Have they ever tried the 48-Hour Rule or experienced the Female Fun-Limitation Factor?

Do they know the 50-50-90 Rule or the meaning of the Cylinder Index? As for the CI the answer is most definitely no, they do not. The place is advertised as a carefree experience, which in my case means that I pay a monthly fee to avoid doing what I would have wanted to do in the first place. We don't blow snow, cut grass, trim weeds, edge the sidewalk, till the garden, or prune shrubs. That's six absent cylinders right there. The list of what I don't have to do is endless.

And for me, hopeless.

I can't walk down the block to the Knack Hardware and Lounge or hit nine-irons into Two Cycle Creek or turn my change into folding money at the Common Surface Savings & Loan. I am a stranger in a strange land, edgy, anxious, no escapes routes to outside or to Mr. Unbelievable's garage.

I miss even the tactile comfort of my old outboard motors, my motorcycles, the anachronistic toggle switches on a vintage Kenwood Model KA-5700 amp and KT-5300 tuner. I miss my music and my collector flashlight guides, my fireworks cabinet, my boating photos of the kids: a great shot of a kid wearing a mask, sanding mahogany in the garage next to the alley, the kid looking up and grinning under the mask.

With time to spare I have visited the old garages, usually on a scooter. As a row-house man, an urban man, it seems like the green thing to do, putter around town on a scooter, seventy-five miles to the gallon.

Number one is long gone, and most who ever set foot in it are long gone as well.

Number two is located on a walking route I have through the city's hilly neighborhoods. One day the owner saw me and started up a conversation. I told him I used to live in his house. He gave me a tour. The common driveway still separates his house from where the Mahoneys used to live, the two one-stall garages still back there against the hedgerow and lilac bushes.

Number three is abutted by the formal public beach that Henry always anticipated. In the days of gaz it was a village beach with a dirt parking lot and featured a long dock with a big, wooden diving tower. If you lived in the village you could get a brass dog tag to use at the beach, but I never saw that anybody checked for them. Everybody knew everybody else, or thought they did. It was a small town.

Today it is paved place with a new brick building for restrooms. The old dock has been replaced by slips for about a dozen boats. Not many swimmers these days.

I'll tell you what, though. When I let my imagination loose I can still hear the musicals and the thump of that magnificent bass drum. I can hear the lawn mowers, and best of all I can hear the old man saying, "We need some gaz."

Gaz, man.

Number four is holding up under that oddly constructed roof. But the CP was ahead of the curve. We had to leave. We had outgrown the house, and I had to quit pretending I was the captain of anything, much less the alley, still narrow and crowned, by the way.

I visit the new garage going up. One night in the dead of winter I stood in the new garage and stared up at the heavens through the roof trusses and thought, this is it, this is the last garage.

Appendices

Frequently Asked Questions from the Garage Logic Radio Show Archives

Q: Is there a 10-run rule in Garage Logic?

A: No. Scores are kept in running totals for all sports played in Garage Logic. There was some grumbling in Euphoria after the University of Garage Logic beat the College of Self Esteem 98-0 in football, but we will not change our policy.

Q: What are those two rules again for duct tape and WD-40?

A: If it moves and it shouldn't, use duct tape. If it doesn't move and it should, use WD-40.

Q: What are sliders, slammers, and floaters?

A: Children. In the days before you needed a degree in physics to strap a kid into an automobile infant seat, kids slid, slammed, and floated around inside the family station wagon. The only thing that kept a kid from sliding, slamming, or floating into the dashboard was the driver's, usually dad's, right arm and hand extended horizontally at each stop sign or red light. Rebuffed, the kid floated back to the seating and cargo area.

Q: What is the difference between an End of the World and It's Almost Over?

A: An End of the World is a report of behavior in Liberal Lakes or Euphoria that at least offers a glimmer of amusement—six-year-olds with cell phones, for example.

An EOW graduates to an it's Almost Over when the behavior reported is so dire as to suggest that life as we know it really is almost over—kids wearing helmets, for example, while playing badminton.

Q: What does Good Luck mean?

A: Aside from its normal applications it means all the best to those of us in the fight to preserve a United States whose traditions and history we appreciate and understand. Good Luck, we're up against something.

Q: What is a Ray of Hope?

A: Anything that defies the Mystery—singing Christmas carols, for example—in a public school without the intervention of the American Civil Liberties Union.

Q: Who is Alvin Straight?

A: Alvin Straight, a World War II vet, farmer, and laborer, drove a 1966 John Deere lawn tractor 240 miles from Laurens, Iowa, to Mount Zion, Wisconsin, in the summer of 1994 to see his estranged brother, Henry, with whom he hadn't spoken in ten years. The trip took six weeks at a top speed of five mph. Alvin was seventy-three at the time.

As a result of his journey and his choice of transportation, Straight is a hero of Garage Logicians, and a statue in his honor is on the east lawn outside the Mower Museum in downtown Garage Logic.

Q: Is it okay to call a CI Girl a Garage Logicianette?

A: I wouldn't. Anything with an ette on it is usually something less than the real thing.

Q: What is a GLA?

A: Anybody over fifty is a GLA, a Great Living American.

Q: How did it come about that young married couples in Garage Logic are advised to tie the Christmas tree to something for the first six years of marriage?

A: During the first six years of marriage both the husband and the wife think they know best how the tree should look, and it tends to get so overloaded with ornaments that it keels over about two nights after its installation. Tying the tree to, say, a windowsill, gets the couple through the rough years until the husband finally backs out of the ritual altogether except for hauling the tree and sawing a fresh cut.

Q: How did Patrick Reusse first get called Oatmeal Ass?

A: On April 13, 1998, when Reusse was supposed to call the show from Augusta, Georgia, on the Monday following one of the most exciting Masters golf tournaments in years, which he covered, he decided to take a flight out of Atlanta instead. I wished upon him a horrible flight, wedged between two female basketball coaches, nothing to read, crying babies all around him, and with the baby in back of him drooling wet oatmeal down his back so that he was sitting in oatmeal for three hours.

At his annual State Fair appearance in 1998 Reusse arrived with a can of oatmeal taped to his ass.

Q: What is the helmet helmet?

A: On April 21, 1998, a guy told us he was hurt by a helmet that fell off a shelf in his garage, and he said he needed a helmet helmet.

Q: What is plate management?

A: At any good feed, especially, for example, Thanksgiving, the seasoned eating veterans in Garage Logic demonstrate a dexterity that allows them, by correct loading, heaping, and stacking, to get more on their plate in one pass through the line than anybody else in the room.

Q: And the role of the nap?

A: Those same seasoned veterans have the uncanny ability to nap through the often-clamorous kitchen cleanup, only to awaken just in time for pie and one more ice-cold beer.

Q: What is the decoy stash?

A: The decoy stash is what used to be the main stash until it gets discovered and tapped into by other people in the house. Once the stash is discovered it becomes the decoy, as you must develop a new real stash while leaving a little something in what is now the decoy.

Q: Are there beer rules in the garage?

A: Just the usual. Garage beer is free to visitors, but they may not dismiss the brand.

Q: Who is Norbert Wiener?

A: He is a famous mathematician, invoked on occasion because the mayor is not.

Q: Do Garage Logicians recycle?

A: If there's anything left and no other uses for what gets recycled.

Q: Is there any counseling in the Garage Logic schools for test anxiety?

A: No.

Q: Does Garage Logic celebrate Earth Day?

A: No. Garage Logicians do, however, celebrate Last Drop Days, with various competitions designed to showcase the value of getting to that last drop.

Q: Who are the CP and DA?

A: The CP is the Chief Procurer and the DA is the Domestic Associate.

Q: What are the guidelines for riding a motorcycle twelve months year in northern climes?

A: A legitimate ride has been determined to be twenty miles. You can't ride around the block one Saturday in January and count that as having accomplished a ride in January.

Q: What is a Failed Superhero?

A: Failed Superheroes, such as Spandex Man or Static Man, have unusual qualities that might be used for the good of humanity, crime fighting, and rescuing damsels in distress, but instead only get them trouble with the law. Failed Superheroes identified to date are: Spandex Man, The Tickler, The Fondler, Toe Sucker, Static Man, The Licker, Sock Man, Tick Man, Werewolf Man, Captain Planet (Al Gore), The Fixer, Bussie, and Golf Cart Man.

Q: What is the Samer Theory?

A: There was a fellow in the military in the 1970s, last name of Samer, who, as a result of working in the communications field, predicted that people would go nuts from all the radioactivity in the air. That he made this prediction before the cell phone was all the more impressive.

Q: Has the Lake Detective ever been stumped?

A: No.

Q: What is doodling?

A: It is the horrible practice of spelling conventional names unconventionally, apparently for the purpose of assigning some sort of noteworthy or celebrity status to a child.
    Examples: "Aaryn" for Erin, "Kaycee" for Casey, and "Brittnye" for Brittany.

Q: Who are the Dark People?

A: Urban residents who wish to dim city lighting at night because they now live in the cities and are in complete denial of the city's role—bright beacons of commerce—in the history and traditions of American life.

Q: What is meant by "the country's tallest buildings?"

A: Big cities. The closer you get to the country's tallest buildings, the more likely you are to find liberal politics, Dark People, and Mysterians.

Foghorn Dictionary

Foghornable word: Any once perfectly useful word that has lost its original meaning due to the inability of opinion makers, politicians, and academics to speak plainly or with conviction, lest they be thought judgmental. These words, when heard by a Garage Logician, are foghorned, as a warning that the English language is perilously close to dashing against the beachhead.

Appropriate: This is the word that started it all. *Appropriate* used to mean "correct" or "acceptable," as in "bond the two pieces of wood using the appropriate glue."

Insidiously, it has replaced "right," just as *inappropriate* has replaced "wrong."

Body Image: Body Image? You might see the image of a body in a photograph. In all other instances give it the foghorn.

Bonding: Bonding is the correct application of epoxy to join two pieces of wood. Bonding has nothing to do with relationships.

Bridge Building: Architects, engineers, and riveters build bridges. Politicians don't.

Closure: You mean "done." You don't ever bring closure to the rebuilding of small-block Chevrolet V8, nor do you need closure at the end of a legislative session. You get done.

Coalition: See "community."

Community: It's right up there with *appropriate* and *inappropriate* as the most foghornable word in the garage or anywhere. *Community* once meant your neighborhood or town. It is now the favorite word of any group of people who identify with each other for the purpose of sustaining what they believe to be victim status. A personal favorite? The Hollywood community. Right. The word is so widely distorted that virtually everybody is a member of a community, especially if they are looking for money, cellists, ranchers, teachers, immigrants, marine scientists, global warming mongers.
   Note: There is no Garage Logic Community.

Connectivity: Conductivity, maybe, but connectivity should never be uttered.

Consensus: It now means what groups of people who don't know what they are talking about reach when they arrive at the worst possible conclusion, usually to imagined problems.

Dialogue: There is dialogue in a play, but in all other cases the word is *conversation.*

Diversity: God only knows what this has come to mean. Misused by people who confuse value for fact. Diversity is a fact; it has no inherent value.
   There is a diversity community, incidentally, which is two foghorns.

Doodled Names. Conventional names spelled incorrectly.

Empower: This gets foghorned because it is used when the government is thought to grant a privilege or power to somebody who already has that privilege or power. The government cannot empower a woman; she is already a woman.

Enable: Hey! Buck up! You either can or you can't.

Facilitate: Did it ever have a legitimate meaning? It now means to fix or arrange, or, most likely, to babysit, usually adults.

Fair: To whom? And who decides?

Green: It used to mean color. Now it means a lifestyle.

Guzzle: What SUVs do to gasoline.

Human Resources: No, you mean *personnel*.

Iconic: When used by critics to describe an artist or a performance, it means that you weren't smart enough to know that.

Inappropriate: See *appropriate*.

Journal: A solid example of a once-useful word that has been stolen by people who cannot write to describe what they are doing with a pen in their hand.

Kindness Retreat: Schoolese for yet another day spent out of the classroom.

Learner: Apparently this sounds less demanding than *student* or *pupil*.

Level the Playing Field: What you do when you are laying out a ball diamond. Anything else gets the foghorn because it is a transparent cry for help to the government to account for failure.

Model: What we used to make out of plastic. Now used by people who believe you can make behavior by merely following instructions. Behavior, of course, is not modeled. It is learned.

Nuance: Of the billions of people in the world, what only George W. Bush was incapable of.

Nurture: Mothers and zookeepers nurture young ones. Ideas don't get nurtured, especially not by politicians, who are only trying to bring about consensus anyway.

Partner: Sounded good in the cowboy movies when summoning a buddy to saddle up. Now means sharing even basic responsibilities so that there are more parties to blame if something goes wrong.

Politically Correct: There is no such thing.

Proactive: The advance warning that a politician intends to horn in early on.

Scary: The word is now meaningless. Everything is scary: traffic, rain, trans fats, barking dogs, secondhand smoke, gas-guzzling SUVs.

Self-Esteem: An appraisal, usually false, of one's self-worth.

Share: An imposition by the government on you, to make the life of your neighbor better.

Skill: Should only be used for learned crafts, like plumbing or carpentry. Blast that horn when you hear somebody say they teach life skills.

Spew: A favorite of newspaper reporters who cannot write "SUV" in a sentence without also including the chunks of pollution they spew out the tailpipe.

Sustainable: Anything favored by environmentalists to inhibit growth.

Totally: See scary. Everything is totally.

Validate: While it is true that an attendant might need to validate a parking ticket, it is unnecessary to validate an opinion or emotion.

Wellness: What we are supposed to be seeking above all else and are victimized, presumably by Big Tobacco or Big Food, when we do not achieve it.

The Garage Logic Song

words and music by Glen Everhart
written in honor of Joe Soucheray, Mayor, Garage Logic, MN

In Gumption County, near Diversityville
There's a place the boys can hang out still
Where common sense is the law of the land
And a beer fits nicely into a man's hand
Where sound advice is given out everyday
By the mayor of town, Joe Soucheray

Garage Logic, mmmmm, Garage Logic
Listen in everyday to what Joe has to say
Garage Logic

Cheer for the fighting Stogies at the University
Where you can take a course in personal responsibility
And you can fish from shore over on Spoon Lake
With your neighbor who showed you how to fix your brakes
Creature Path Golf Course has a cheap green fee
And you can tee it up with Joe Soucheray

chorus

So take a ride on your Harley, it ain't very far
And head into town, and light up a cigar
Find your buddy's garage, turn on the radio
And tune into the Joe Soucheray Show
Or put your feet up and kick back in your chair
The Garage Logic show is on the air!

chorus

About the Author

Columnist and radio show host Joe Soucheray is the author of several books, including *Waterline: Of Fathers, Sons, and Boats*, *Once there was a ballpark: The season of the Met, 1956–1981*, a reminiscence about Metropolitan Stadium; *Sooch! Sports writing of Joe Soucheray of the Minneapolis Tribune; Modern, Caring, Sensitive Male: A Curmudgeon Columnist Looks at Life*; and several books in the series Creative Education Sports Superstars. He was a sports columnist for the *Minneapolis Tribune* before he joined the *St. Paul Pioneer Press*.

Soucherary has been the host of *Garage Logic* since 1993, where he serves as mayor and fireworks commissioner. The show is broadcast from KSTP-AM 1500 in St. Paul and heard on twenty-two affiliates.

Not entirely surrounded by Euphorians, but close, Soucheray and his wife Jennifer live in St. Paul, Minnesota.

About the Artist

Greg Holcomb is a system field technician for Excel Energy, meaning he fixes things that break in substations, including nuclear plants. His cartoons have appeared in newspapers and magazines, and on billboards, cards, and business-to-business promotions. Holcomb, his wife Laurie, and daughter Jessi live in South Minneapolis, surrounded by Euphorians.

Acknowledgements

My thanks to Rookie, Angie, John Heidt, Kenny Olson, Pat Reusse, John Camp, Dan Kelly, Terry Cullen, and the Hubbard family.